THAT WILDER BOY

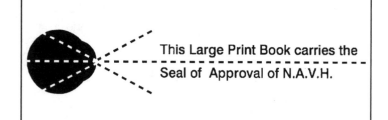

This Large Print Book carries the
Seal of Approval of N.A.V.H.

KANSAS WEDDINGS, BOOK 2

THAT WILDER BOY

THE TRIALS OF MODERN LIFE
MAKE WAY FOR ROMANCE

KIM VOGEL SAWYER

THORNDIKE PRESS
A part of Gale, Cengage Learning

Detroit • New York • San Francisco • New Haven, Conn • Waterville, Maine • London

GALE
CENGAGE Learning

LIBRARY OF CONGRESS CATALOGING-IN-PUBLICATION DATA

Sawyer, Kim Vogel.
  That Wilder boy : the trials of modern life make way for romance / By Kim Vogel Sawyer.
    p. cm. — (Kansas weddings ; bk. 2) (Thorndike Press large print Christian fiction)
    ISBN-13: 978-1-4104-1227-0 (hardcover : alk. paper)
    ISBN-10: 1-4104-1227-X (hardcover : alk. paper)
    1. Man-woman relationships—Fiction. 2. Kansas—Fiction. I. Title.
PS3619.A97T43 2009
813'.6—dc22   2008042339

Published in 2009 by arrangement with Barbour Publishing, Inc.

Printed in the United States of America
1 2 3 4 5 6 7 12 11 10 09 08

For Kristian, who believes the most
"tarnished" life can be made shiny and
new.

Dear Reader,

Welcome to Kansas, home of my birth! In my 40-some years of life I have lived all but one year in the heart of America's breadbasket, and I can't imagine living anywhere else. Creating my own Kansas town and peopling it with special friends has been a great deal of fun.

The character of John was inspired by a man who attends my church. John's favorite seat is the bench right in front of our sound booth. It gives him a straight view to the minister's pulpit, and from the choir loft, I've had a straight view of John. Every emotion can be read in John's face, and his sincere, heartfelt worship has moved me to tears on more than one occasion. He's taught me a great deal about throwing off one's inhibitions and praising God with the whole heart, so it gives me great pleasure to share John with you in these stories.

I hope you enjoy the visit to Kansas as much as I enjoy living here. Please feel free to visit my Web site at www.KimVogel Sawyer.com and drop me a note — I love to hear from readers!

May God bless you richly
as you journey with Him,
Kim Vogel Sawyer

ONE

Carrie Mays hung the little cardboard OUT TO LUNCH sign on the door handle of the manager's office and stepped into the bright August sunshine. Her lunch bag in one hand and a romance novel in the other, she moved briskly around Tower One, which housed the office, and made her way to the grassy courtyard.

For a moment she stood and perused the area surrounded by the six apartment towers then chose a bench directly in the center where an ornamental flowering tree provided an umbrella of dappled shade. Settling on the bench, she crossed her legs, opened her paper lunch bag, and withdrew her sandwich. She hummed as she unzipped the plastic baggy and removed the tuna salad sandwich. Lowering her head, she offered a brief prayer then raised the sandwich to her lips.

Just as she took the first bite, a strange

rattle sounded from somewhere behind her. Puzzled, she peeked over her shoulder. Unable to determine the source of the sound, she shrugged and turned her attention back to her sandwich.

The rattle became a *rat-tat-tat,* and then something cold slapped her across the back. With a startled shriek she leaped from the bench, knocking her lunch bag to the ground. She spun around in time for a second slap of water to catch her in the front, right across her knees, soaking the hem of her capris.

"W–what?" For a moment she remained rooted in place, unable to process what was happening. But as the arc of water came at her again, she realized the watering system on the north half of the courtyard had come to life. At noon? She jumped backward, avoiding another blast of water, but to her chagrin her book, which still lay on the bench, took a solid hit.

"Oh no!" She waited for the arc to move on, snatched up her book and lunch bag, then dashed for safety on the sidewalk next to Tower Two. She stood, dripping, holding her sodden sandwich and book away from her body and shaking her head in disbelief at this disruption of her peaceful lunch.

A man trotted around from behind Tower

Three and stopped at the edge of the sidewalk. Carrie watched him shield his eyes as he surveyed the area. A smile grew on his face, and he socked the air, releasing an exultant "Yes!" The word carried clearly across the expanse of grass to her ears.

"Yes!"? She felt her fury mounting. Had he turned on the system at noon? Her notes said watering was to be done from five to six-thirty in the morning, not at noon. So what was that "yes!" all about? She started to call to him, but he turned and jogged behind the building.

In a few moments a stuttering chop-chop-chop then hisssss signaled the shutdown of the sprinklers. Water droplets glistened on blades of grass like tiny diamonds. Carrie stared for a moment at the grass, waiting to see if the system would spring to life again. When it didn't, she stomped down the sidewalk, her anger increasing with every step in her squishy sandals, to the place where the man had disappeared. She rounded the corner of Tower Three at a good clip and collided full force with a solid chest.

"Ack!" The force knocked the book from her hand and bounced her backward two feet. Dirty hands caught her upper arms, keeping her from falling on her seat. The

11

moment she had her footing, she jerked loose and opened her mouth to let loose a tirade.

"What're you doing, running down the sidewalk like that?" The man's scolding voice cut off Carrie's words. "You could get hurt, especially when the sidewalk's wet. That makes it slippery."

Carrie's jaw dropped. *He* was chastising *her?* Without answering his question she posed one of her own. "And just why *is* the sidewalk wet?" She swung her soggy lunch bag in the direction of the courtyard. "Since when do we run the watering system in the middle of the day?"

The man took one step backward and crossed his arms. Muscular arms, Carrie noted, tanned from the shoulders of his sleeveless T-shirt to his knobby knuckles. She swallowed and drew herself to her full height — which was minimal compared to his; he was so tall! — then threw back her head in a pretense of haughtiness to disguise the sudden quivering in her belly. "I asked you a question. Why was the watering system turned on at noon? It's clearly against policy."

A muscle in the man's jaw twitched as his gaze roved from the waterlogged bag in her hand to her dripping capris. In a low drawl he answered, "This morning at five o'clock, according to policy" — he had the audacity to offer a teasing smirk — "when I ran the system I noticed one of the sprinklers wasn't working. So . . . I replaced the head. I had to turn things on to make sure that's what the problem was. I was hoping it wasn't underground, in the line. Pretty big relief to me to see it working."

So he was the groundskeeper, Carrie realized. He had a valid reason for running the system, but still. . . . "But still, couldn't you look before you turn things on? I was right out there on that bench, and getting wet was a rather unpleasant surprise." She gestured toward her capris. The linen was beginning to dry, turning into a crunch of wrinkles around her knees.

He glanced at her clothes then stooped over and picked up her book. He examined it for a moment, his lips tucking in as he ran his thumb across the damp, curling pages. Holding out the book on his broad hand, he met her gaze squarely. She noticed his eyes were a deep brown with very thick, curling lashes. Lashes most women would love to have. But they did nothing to downplay his rugged masculinity. She felt a blush building.

"I did look, but you weren't there at the

time. You must've come out when I was behind the building. I'm really sorry." He raised his wide shoulders in a boyish shrug. "Maybe I didn't look closely enough. Rarely are any of the residents in the courtyard at noon — they're all inside eating."

His calm, penitent reply deflated Carrie's anger. She snatched the book from his hand and hugged it against her chest. "It's okay. I'll dry. It just surprised me is all."

A low chuckle emitted from his throat. "Yeah, I imagine." His gaze dropped to her soggy sandwich. "Can I replace your lunch?" He jerked his thumb toward Tower One. "There are some snack machines in the lobby — nothing fancy, but you won't go hungry."

Carrie backed up two slow steps. "No. No, thank you. I–I'm going to need to run home and change my clothes."

He followed, advancing the same two steps, a lazy smile on his handsome face. "So you'll be back?"

Carrie nodded, the movement rapid and jerky. Why was she feeling so . . . discombobulated? "Yes. I'm filling in as office manager while Jim's on vacation." She reversed another slow step.

He advanced another slow step. "Ah. So I'll see you around?" The idea seemed to

14

please him.

It pleased her, too. "I suppose so, if you're here every day." She stopped moving backward.

He stopped, too, and stuck his hands into the pockets of his well-worn jeans. "I'm here every day. I'm Rocky."

She shook her head. "You're — what?"

He laughed softly, a pleasant sound. "Rocky. That's my name. Robert Jr., really, but I've always been called Rocky." He paused, tipping his head, the sun bringing out glints of yellow in his tousled brown locks. "And you are — ?"

"Carrie." She allowed a grin to tip up her lips. "Caroline, really, but I've always been called Carrie."

A full smile grew on his face, exposing white teeth, the front two slightly overlapped. Dimples appeared in his honed cheeks, causing Carrie's heart to skip a beat. "Carrie. It's nice to meet you."

"You, too, Rocky." They stood for a silent minute, smiling at one another. Then Carrie jerked to attention. "I–I've got to go. I'll need to open the office again by one."

He nodded. "Better scoot then. Take care, Carrie. I'll see you around."

"Yes. . . ." Why was her breathing so erratic? Blowing out a big breath, she said,

"Good-bye, Rocky." She spun and trotted to the office where she retrieved her purse, climbed in her car and headed for home. She resisted the urge to look back and see if Rocky was watching.

Rocky watched Carrie slide gracefully behind the wheel of a compact sports car, the layers of her long blond hair swinging forward to hide her profile from view. He swallowed as she tucked the hair behind her ear, revealing the sweet curve of her jaw. Pretty girl. Really pretty girl.

And very nice car. . . .

He watched until the car left the grounds then turned back toward the tool shack. The car settled it. Carrie was out of his league. He'd thought as much when he'd seen the outfit she was wearing. All the beadwork on the top and around the cuffs of the pants gave her away. She didn't shop discount stores. Still, he hadn't been able to resist flirting a little bit.

Flirting came naturally. He admitted it without a hint of bigheadedness as he placed the tools in their spots on the peg-board. Girls usually thought he was good looking. There'd been a time when he used that to his advantage, but — and a rush of pleasure washed over him — he'd learned not to use people like that anymore.

Six months ago he'd given his heart to Jesus. And ever since he'd been working at replacing the bad habits with things from the Bible. He didn't use girls anymore. But he did enjoy a little healthy flirting. He hoped Jesus didn't mind.

The tool shack back in order, he grabbed his lunch box and headed for the courtyard, to the bench where Carrie'd been sitting. The concrete bench was dry to the touch, but darker gray showed where the spatter of water had struck.

He couldn't help smiling, thinking about how that cold water must have shocked the wind out of Carrie's lungs. Then he stifled his amusement, remembering the ruined book. He sure would like to replace it. He wracked his brain. What was the title? *Loyal . . . Something.* And the author? Marie . . . Somebody. He released a huff of aggravation. He'd seen similar books somewhere recently.

Ah! He slapped his thigh as remembrance dawned. In Eileen Cassidy's apartment. She had a whole shelf full of romance books. He looked toward Tower Three's fifth floor. He knew she'd welcome his company, and she probably had a full cookie jar. Decision made, he jumped up and headed for Tower Three.

Eileen answered his knock on the third tap. As he suspected, she offered a huge smile and waved him in. "Just in time for lunch! I've got some corned beef and Swiss on rye and some store-bought potato salad. Help yourself." She settled herself at the kitchen bar and pointed to the stool beside her. "Climb up."

"Are you sure?" Rocky stood beside the bar, the sight of the towering sandwich inviting him to dive in.

Eileen nodded. "I made an extra one for John, but he said he'd be going for a hamburger for lunch. So I've got a spare."

That was all the prompting Rocky needed. He sat. "Thanks." He offered a brief prayer then lifted the hefty sandwich. "Corned beef and Swiss sounds a lot better than my bologna."

"Bologna. Phooey. Give it to Roscoe." Eileen laughed as her huge yellow and white cat, who lazed in a spot of sunshine in the middle of the living room, lifted his head and chirped a *"brow?"* in response to her suggestion.

Rocky liked Eileen. She was really more his brother Philip's friend. She had worked at Philip's job placement service for disabled adults before becoming a resident caretaker here at Elmwood Towers. But in the past months she had adopted him as well. Eileen adopted everybody, Rocky thought as he bit into the thick sandwich. He still had a little trouble relating to her boys, as she called the three adults with developmental delays who were in her charge, but his Bible said he was to treat people the way he wanted to be treated. All people. And he was trying.

"So what're you up to today?" Eileen asked, working her words around a bite.

Rocky propped his elbows on the edge of the bar, wiping away a bit of mustard with his knuckle. "Fixed the watering system this morning — bad sprinkler head. This afternoon I've got to mow the north yard and the courtyard and do some weeding around your flower beds."

Eileen grinned. "Flowers are blooming like crazy, aren't they?"

"Yeah. But they sure create extra work for me." He grinned to let her know he wasn't complaining.

She laughed and nudged him with her elbow. "Aw, they're worth it. The boys and I are scoping out the grounds, looking for new places to plant. We want to add a garden or two every year. Might even try to bury some daffodil or tulip bulbs yet for a nice surprise next spring."

"Well, let me clear the spots for you when you find them, okay? Digging up that sod is too hard for you." The protectiveness caught Rocky by surprise. He remembered a time when he wouldn't have cared if an old lady worked too hard.

"I'll do that. But you will let the boys and me plant the flowers, won't you?"

Rocky nodded. "Sure." He finished his sandwich.

Eileen pointed into the kitchen. "Cookie jar's full."

He grinned. "Thanks." He ambled around the corner, pulled out two good-sized chocolate chip cookies then headed back toward the bar. His gaze lit on the bookshelf that stood on the north wall of Eileen's living room. A row of short paperback novels drew him like a magnet. In four steps he was in front of the shelf.

A chuckle sounded from beside him. Eileen stood at his elbow. "What are you looking at?"

He tapped one book with his finger. "These. You sure have a bunch of them."

Eileen nodded. "Yes. Ro-o-o-omances." She sighed the word, clasping her wrinkled hands beneath her chin and fluttering her eyelashes.

Rocky laughed, shaking his head. Who'd have thought romance still bloomed in the hearts of old ladies?

Eileen quirked a brow. "*You* don't read romances, do you?"

"No." He scanned the titles. "But I need one." Briefly he explained the morning's catastrophe and shared what he could remember of the book's title.

Eileen's eyebrows shot up. "Oh! One of my favorites — *Loyal Traitor.* I think Marie Harrison wrote that one." Eileen trailed her finger along the spines then crowed, "Yep! Right here." She pulled the book from its spot and held it out. "Is this it?"

"Yeah!" Rocky licked a bit of chocolate from his finger and took the book. "Can I buy this from you?"

Eileen shrugged, crossing to the sofa and sinking into the cushions. Roscoe immediately jumped in her lap. She petted the cat with one hand and flapped the other hand in his direction. "Take it."

Rocky hesitated. "But you said it's one of your favorites."

Eileen chuckled. "As you can see I have a shelf full. I'll survive. Besides, if you're going to dig up a spot of sod for me, you'll earn the price of that book."

Rocky shook the book at her. "Thanks.

Appreciate it." He glanced at his wristwatch and sighed. "I gotta get back to work."

Eileen pushed the purring cat from her lap and rose to walk him to the door. She gave him a quick hug before opening the door for him. "Enjoy your afternoon. And I hope the book does the trick."

Rocky turned back. "The trick?"

Eileen smirked. "Uh-huh. I saw the light in your eyes when you mentioned the girl on the bench."

Rocky felt heat climb his neck. "Oh, but —"

Eileen shook her finger at him. "Don't start that with me. I'm old, but I'm not stupid."

Rocky ducked his head, fighting the urge to smile. "Come on, Eileen. . . ."

She laughed and gave him another impulsive hug. "She could do worse! Now go get that book delivered and get your mowing done." She shooed him out the door.

"She could do worse. . . ." Eileen's words replayed themselves in Rocky's head as he stepped into the elevator. Who would have imagined someone saying that about Rocky Wilder, the troublemaker from the wrong side of the tracks? He punched the lobby button and felt the car begin its descent. As much as Eileen's words touched him, he

knew his limitations. Carrie was obviously not within his reach. He tapped his leg with the book. He'd make amends for ruining her novel; then he'd forget about her. She was only filling in for two weeks. It would be easy to forget her.

The elevator came to a stop, and he headed back to the courtyard. As he crossed the grass toward Tower One, a splash of pink and white caught his eye. Eileen's impatiens. Impulsively he veered to the right and pinched off a few blooms. The flowers would make up for her ruined lunch.

He'd make amends then forget her. Easy.

Yeah, right. . . .

Two

Her wristwatch showed a quarter after one when Carrie zipped into the reserved parking space at Elmwood Towers. Stepping from the air-conditioned interior of the car into the August heat was a shock, but within minutes she entered the manager's office and drew in a breath of cool air — apple-scented, thanks to the little plug-in air freshener she'd brought yesterday. Her sundress swirled around her ankles as she moved to the desk and set down her purse next to a wilting cluster of pink and white blossoms that rested on top of —

She straightened in surprise and looked around. Someone had been in here! And the only "someones" who had a key for this office, other than her, were the owners, the maintenance manager, and the groundskeeper.

The groundskeeper. Rocky. Of course.

Her heart turned a little somersault as she

envisioned his tan, long-fingered hands plucking those delicate blossoms and arranging them into a little bouquet. Turning to the desk, she lifted the flowers to her nose then picked up the book. The flowers were obviously from the courtyard, but where could he have gotten the book? She had no idea, but she couldn't believe how special it made her feel to think he had gone to that trouble. How long had it been since someone had done something so unexpectedly sweet for her? Not since Carl.

The happy lift in her heart plummeted as she thought of Carl. Even after two years it stung to remember how hopelessly in love she'd fallen only to discover Carl's kindness was meant to win her trust fund, not her heart. With a sigh she pushed aside thoughts of Carl and focused on the pink and white bouquet.

The poor little petals drooped. Maybe a drink would refresh them. She hoped so. She walked to the kitchenette and scrounged around for a plastic cup which she filled with water. Then she arranged the flowers in the cup. They spilled over the cup's brim in a haphazard manner, but she didn't care. Returning to the office area, she cleared the corner of the desk and placed the flowers where they'd receive a splash of afternoon sun.

Funny how cheerful the whole room seemed with the addition of the flower bouquet. As she worked, her gaze often drifted to the flowers, and each time her heart gave that same happy lift. Around two thirty she heard the rev of a lawn mower starting up — *Rocky* — and she nearly jumped out of her seat to race to the window. But just as her palms pressed the desk top, ready to push herself from the chair, good sense took over.

How ridiculous would she look, running to the window for a peek at the gardener? The man accidentally ruined her lunch and her book — and he made a simple gesture of apology. She shouldn't read any more into it than that. The last thing she needed was for him to get the wrong idea.

She kept herself in her seat, but as the mower's motor volume increased, indicating the mower was moving closer, she couldn't help straining upward to peer out for a glimpse of him as the machine went by. And as it passed the window he turned his head and caught her looking.

She jerked her gaze back to the desk top where it collided with the romance novel. Her heart rate increased to double-time. *RRRRRRRrrrrrrrrr.* . . . The mower moved on.

But her pulse didn't slow. She pressed her hand to her chest and said, "Stop it! Just get busy here."

And she tried. But when she heard the mower's approach — *rrrrrrrRRRRRRR* — she couldn't resist another peek. Sure enough — he looked, too. And this time he smiled.

She smiled back. She couldn't stop herself. Then she looked away, certain her face flamed red even through her tanning booth bronze. *RRRRRRRrrrrrrrr. . . .* The mower and its rider moved beyond her sight. She stuck out her lower lip and blew, ruffling her bangs. Enough of this now! Determinedly she set her attention on the rent receipts. But the mower's coming and going continued to disrupt her focus.

Rocky couldn't hold back his grin. He'd seen Carrie's big blue eyes peeking through that window as he went by on the mower. And he'd seen her face break into a smile.

She'd found the book and flowers. And she appreciated them.

Felt really good to do something nice like that. When he looked back on his life, he couldn't find too many instances of doing good. He'd terrorized smaller kids in grade school, hungry for the power bullying brought. In junior high and early high school he'd run with a rough crowd and had gotten into more than his fair share of trouble from vandalism to breaking curfew. But not until he got caught stealing did he figure out the consequences weren't worth the risk. He'd quit breaking the law, but he'd never really grasped the idea of doing good deeds. Instead, he'd remained a bully. Made his heart ache now, thinking of how many people he had hurt with his actions.

He sure wished it hadn't taken him twenty-nine years to figure out doing good brought more pleasure than causing trouble, but at least he was finally there. Now he had a lot of making up to do. Funny how God had plunked him here at Elmwood Towers, right where one of the people he'd wronged was living.

In his mind he could still see the teenaged John's trusting face, expecting Rocky to offer assistance when he needed it, but instead Rocky had played a dirty trick. At the time he'd thought it was funny, causing the disabled boy to look like a fool, but now? His grip tightened on the steering wheel. As uncomfortable as it made him to be around John and the reminder of how mean he'd been, he was glad for the opportunity to set things right. He whispered a prayer for John right then, that the man would have a good day at work and no one would do anything unkind to him. It felt good to talk to God so easily, too.

Rocky slowed the mower to maneuver around the rock border of one of Eileen's garden plots, and the sight of those flowers reminded him of his promise to dig up another garden spot for her. A grin tugged at his cheeks. That Eileen — she sure was something, friends with everybody. He could learn some lessons from her on being Christlike, that's for sure.

He straightened the mower again, aiming it past the office's window. His attention immediately reverted to the girl in the office. Would Carrie step out, flag him down, thank him for the book and flowers? His hopeful gaze drifted to the window, but this time Carrie didn't even look up as he went by.

He blew out a breath of discouragement and thumped the steering wheel with the heel of his hand. That was the problem with a mindless task like mowing — it let a person's mind wander too much. What was he doing thinking about Carrie anyway? He had no business sneaking glances at someone like her. She was obviously quality. Quality wasn't a word anyone would attach to Rocky. Not even Eileen in her kindest moment.

The mower made a final swing through the center of the courtyard. Out of the corner of his eye he caught a glimpse of a floral sundress. Against his will his head swivelled in that direction. Sure enough, it was Carrie. His heart pounded hard under his sweaty T-shirt. Was she waiting to talk to him? But, no, she was moving — heading down the sidewalk toward the parking lot.

He swallowed the lump of disappointment that filled his throat as she climbed into her little car and pulled away without a backward glance. Defeated, Rocky turned his gaze straight ahead. Sure, he was making changes on the inside, but on the outside? He was still rough ol' Rocky Wilder. Nothing but a glorified gardener. His pop had told him he'd never amount to a hill of beans, and in all likelihood Pop was right. His brother, Philip, had been the smart one. Rocky barely squeaked by in high school. Manual labor was all he was good for. Carrie must have seen the truth, too. Why would a girl like that bother with a rough laborer like him?

Just focus on your work, he told himself firmly, wiping sweat that trickled from his forehead. *Remember that verse . . . whatever you do, do it as for the Lord, not for men. Even if it's just gardening, do your best. But quit thinking about impressing some girl who's out of your league. It's a waste of time.*

Carrie sat at the stop sign, letting several opportunities to pull into the flow of traffic escape, while she fingered the copy of *Loyal Traitor* which rested on the console. Guilt pinched her conscience. She should have said thank you. It was rude not to acknowledge a kind gesture. Her mother had certainly taught her manners! Why hadn't she said anything to Rocky?

She knew why. Fear, plain and simple. Rocky was a gardener. Probably didn't make much more than minimum wage. The minute he found out she had money, he'd be after her at full throttle, but not because he liked her. Because he liked her wealth. Maybe he'd already figured it out. After all, everyone in town knew of the Steinwoods. Even though she insisted on using her deceased father's name rather than her stepfather's, it was common knowledge that Carrie Mays was Mac Steinwood's stepdaughter. Between her father's millions and Mac's millions, men looked at Carrie and saw dollar signs. It had happened before. She wouldn't let it happen again.

It didn't matter at all that Rocky set her heart to fluttering as it hadn't fluttered in more than two years. What mattered was that her heart would only be broken if she allowed him in. And Carrie wouldn't suffer through another broken heart.

She removed her foot from the brake and eased into traffic, aiming her car toward home. She drove automatically, her mind refusing to let go of Rocky. What was it about him? He was undeniably handsome with his thick, unruly hair and chiseled features. His boyish smile, with the overlapping front teeth, had a charm that was nearly irresistible. His muscular arms, wide shoulders, and narrow hips spoke of a man who knew how to work hard. That strength appealed to her, she realized. So many of the men her stepfather encouraged her to date used their minds rather than their muscles at their jobs, and most had gotten soft. She couldn't call Rocky soft. The name Rocky fit him well — he seemed as solid as a rock.

Yet there must be a tenderness underneath. Concern had made him scold when she'd run down the wet sidewalk. His penitent expression when he realized he'd ruined her book and her lunch also showcased kindness. He'd offered to replace her lunch, had managed to replace her book, and had even taken the time to pick her some flowers as an apology. Sweet. . . . Despite his rough appearance Rocky was very, very sweet.

Her fingers found the book again, and she caressed the smooth cover, wishing she were running her fingers across the back of Rocky's hand instead.

Stop it! This was ridiculous. She was fantasizing like some love-sick high school girl. How silly to fixate on a man she would likely never see again. Her time at Elmwood Towers would last as long as Jim's vacation — another nine days. Obviously she and Rocky moved in different social circles. She'd be back in graduate school soon, finishing her second degree. Why spend time mooning over someone who would be in and out of her life in a matter of days?

Ridiculous. Absolutely ridiculous.

She pulled up to the gates of the Stein-wood estate, pushed the button to lower the car's window, and punched in the security code on the button pad. The gates obediently swung wide, and she pulled through, following the curving bricked driveway to the four-car garage behind the house. She pushed the remote to open her port in the garage, guided the car into its spot then pushed the remote again to seal herself inside. Opening the car door, she reached for her purse and the book.

The moment her hand closed over the novel, guilt slapped her again. She owed Rocky a thank-you. Not only was it bad manners to ignore his gesture, but it was unchristian as well. She knew the Bible verse about whatever a person did for the least of these was like doing it for God. She had failed her Savior by ignoring Rocky this afternoon.

She lowered her head and offered a brief prayer of apology to God. She then asked Him to help her find a way to apologize to Rocky. "But don't let me lead him on, Lord," she added fervently. "He's too . . . appealing. I don't want to give him the wrong impression. I just want to say I'm sorry. Help him see only an apology in my words, not an invitation to pursue me. I don't want that, Lord!"

Her prayer finished, she left the garage and entered the house through the service porch and into the kitchen. Her favorite scent — cinnamon and apples — greeted her nostrils the moment she stepped through the door, and she sniffed appreciatively, shooting a wide smile at Myrna, the cook.

"Mm, something smells great!" Her gaze located a dozen muffins cooling on a rack on the marble-topped counter. "Are they for anything special? Mom having her book club ladies over or something?"

Myrna returned Carrie's smile, her full cheeks dimpling. "No, Miss Carrie. I bought a bushel of apples this morning, and I've been making pies all afternoon to put in the freezer. I had some leftover slices, so I grated them for muffins. They're still warm. Would you like one now?"

Carrie eagerly reached for a muffin. The crumbly topping of brown sugar and cinnamon melted in her mouth with the first bite. She rolled her eyes and released a groan of pleasure. "Oh, Myrna, these are wonderful!" She licked the cinnamon from her finger and winked. "And I bet you left out the calories, too, right?"

Myrna laughed, and Carrie joined in. But both women kept their voices quiet. Carrie's parents didn't approve of her carrying on with the staff. She finished her muffin while Myrna began stacking dirty mixing bowls in the dishwasher.

"Thanks so much," Carrie said after finishing the last bite. "That was scrumptious."

"You're welcome, Miss Carrie," Myrna

said with a warm smile.

Carrie started to leave the kitchen, but then an idea struck. She spun back to face the cook. "Myrna, if those muffins aren't for anything special, could I possibly have some of them? Maybe a half dozen — or even just four — to take to work tomorrow?"

Myrna shrugged. "Certainly. When they're cool, I'll put them in a container for you. They'll be in the butler's pantry."

Carrie dashed back and gave the sturdy cook a quick hug. "Thanks, Myrna! You're a doll!"

Myrna blushed with pleasure, but she didn't say anything.

Carrie headed for her bedroom, a smile on her lips. Her thank-you would be made in a way sure to please Rocky. And then she could set aside her guilt and forget all about him. But when she placed *Loyal Traitor* on her bedside table, the title suddenly mocked her. Would Rocky prove to be loyal or a traitor if she gave him a chance?

She shook her head, irritated with herself. It seemed apparent her heart would prove to be traitorous when it came to forgetting Rocky.

THREE

Rocky trooped across the still-dewy grass, a spade over one shoulder and a length of garden hose looped through his elbow. He hoped Eileen would be pleased with the area he'd cleared for her tulips and daffodils. His research indicated a sunny area was preferable, so he'd chosen a spot along the walking path behind the Towers, the one that led to the recreation areas.

Instead of clearing a rectangle, he'd laid the hose in a shape that resembled the top of a grand piano, its straight base against the concrete walkway. He'd do some checking and see if he could locate another concrete bench in the storage barn. If he bought a flowering bush and some perennials, the garden would make a pleasant spot for residents to sit and relax from spring through fall. Maybe he could even rig up one of those solar lamps to provide light in the area at night and add a touch of elegance.

Whistling, he rounded the corner toward the tool shed, and something caught his eye. His steps slowed. A little wicker basket with a napkin draped across it hung from a nail in the doorjamb. Where'd that come from? He swung the spade from his shoulder, leaned it against the shed wall and unhooked the basket. Pinching the napkin between his thumb and first finger — his hands were filthy — he lifted the edge of the blue-and-white checkered cloth and peeked inside.

Muffins, shaped like over-sized toadstools, with some sort of crumbly stuff across their tops. He stuck his nose over the basket and sniffed, and the scent of cinnamon tickled his nostrils. Licking his lips in anticipation, he carried the basket into the shed and set it down on a shelf. He hung up the hose and put the spade away then smiled at the basket as he passed it on the way back outside to the hydrant where he washed his hands.

He knew who left them. He'd seen Eileen troop off about an hour ago with her boys, obviously taking them to work. She must have seen him, too, and figured out he was clearing her garden spot. The muffins were her thank-you. Well, as soon as he was cleaned up, he'd head to her apartment and give her a big hug of thanks.

He dried his hands on the seat of his pants, tucked the basket under his arm and headed to Tower Three. He hummed as he rode the elevator to the fifth floor. A knock on Eileen's door brought an immediate response.

"Rocky!" Eileen greeted him. Her cat, Roscoe, hung from her arm. She waved a hand, inviting him in. "Taking a break?"

"I just came to say thanks." He tipped the basket in her direction. "These look great."

Eileen lifted the edge of the napkin and peeked inside. Her eyebrows shot upward. "They do look great." Roscoe tipped his nose toward them, too, so she put the cat down. "But why are you telling me thanks?"

He frowned. "Didn't you leave them for me?"

She shrugged. "Can't blame me. I bake cookies, not muffins." She ran her pudgy finger along the edge of the woven basket. "Besides, I wouldn't package something up that fancy. Baggies or recycled margarine tubs are my containers of choice."

"Oh." He looked into the basket. "I just figured you'd seen me clearing your new garden spot and left me these as a reward."

Eileen put her hands on her hips. "Now wait a minute. That's what the book was for, right?"

Rocky grinned.

"But where'd you put my new spot?"

The eagerness in her voice increased Rocky's eagerness to share it with her. He guided her to the kitchen where he could point out the window. Roscoe followed and rubbed against his leg.

"See along the walking path? I cleared an area big enough to hold a bench as well as a nice flowering shrub — maybe a hydrangea or butterfly bush." He gestured as he spoke, envisioning the finished garden. "I could plant some ground cover, something your tulips and daffodils can pop through, and then after they've bloomed and died out, we could put in some annuals so the garden will keep blooming all through the summer and into fall."

Eileen stared at him in amazement. "Rocky, that sounds wonderful! All I wanted was a few holes to drop bulbs in. I didn't expect a whole landscaped garden."

Rocky shrugged. "Once I got started, the ideas kept growing. I hope that's okay."

"It's more than okay," she said. She crossed her arms, leaned against the counter, and smirked at him. "You've got a knack, young man. You're going to have this place looking so spiffy they'll raise the rent."

He laughed. "Not likely."

"I'm serious, Rocky. You should consider hiring yourself out as a landscaper."

Rocky felt his chest puff with pleasure at her praise. Still, he countered, "You have to go to school if anybody's gonna take you seriously as a landscaper. I couldn't do that."

"Why not?"

He shrugged. There were a number of reasons, funding being a major part of it. But he said, "Too dumb, I guess."

"Nonsense. You should think about it. And *pray* about it. God gives gifts, and He expects us to use 'em." Then she pulled her mouth sideways and added, " 'Course, we didn't solve the mystery of the muffins, did we?"

Rocky looked into the basket again. "No, I guess we didn't."

"Well, I think I can solve it." Eileen crossed to the refrigerator and pulled out a jug of milk. She poured two glasses as she continued. "This morning, when I took the boys to work, we passed the manager's office and waved at that cute little substitute. She was eating a muffin that looked an awful lot like those in the basket."

Rocky felt his ears go hot. "She — she was?"

"Yep." Eileen plunked the two glasses of milk on the kitchen bar and gestured for Rocky to sit. "So my guess is those muffins are a thank-you — but not from me. They're a thank-you from the girl you gave *Loyal Traitor* to yesterday."

Rocky sat down and took a sip of cold milk. Carrie, huh? He felt a smile growing, but he tugged it down with his finger. *Can't read too much into it,* he told himself. Just a you-scratched-my back, I'll-scratch-yours sort of thing. Still, imagining her sneaking over to the tool shed and leaving that little basket made his chest feel tight.

"So can I have one?"

Eileen's voice brought Rocky back to the present. "Huh? Oh . . . sure." He flipped the napkin off the basket. "Go ahead." They each took a muffin and munched in companionable silence while Roscoe moved back and forth between their feet, his gold eyes turned upward in hopefulness.

When Eileen had wiped her hands clean on a paper towel, she turned to Rocky and asked brightly, "So what's your next move?"

Rocky jerked his gaze in her direction. "What?"

She shook her head. "Your next move. It's

your turn, you know. You gave her a book; she gave you muffins. Now it's back to you."

"Oh." Rocky rubbed the back of his neck. "I–I guess maybe I should at least say thanks, huh?"

Eileen nodded. "Yep. You should."

Then something occurred to him. "But what if it wasn't Carrie? I thought it was you, and I was wrong. What if you're wrong? What if whoever gave me the muffins also gave some to Carrie? That could be why you saw her eating one."

Eileen scratched her chin. "I suppose that's a possibility. . . ."

The more he thought about it, the more certain he became. Carrie had just taken off yesterday without so much as a good-bye. Was it likely she'd bake him muffins after ignoring him? But then again maybe the muffins were an I'm-sorry message. Maybe she felt bad about not acknowledging the book. Maybe this was her way of apologizing. . . .

"What're you thinking?" Eileen cut into his thoughts again.

He offered a sheepish grin. "I was just trying to figure out why Carrie might've left them. Assuming she's the one who did."

"Seems obvious to me," Eileen said as she got up and swept the crumbs from the counter into her palm. She headed for the kitchen wastebasket with Roscoe on her heels. "It's a thank-you gesture, pure and simple. 'Course" — she fixed him with a firm look — "there's only one sure-fire way to find out."

He sucked in his breath.

"You just gotta go ask."

Carrie rustled through the file of applications, searching for a blank document. She heard the office door open and felt a brief rush of warm air that activated the apple scent from the air freshener. Without turning around she said, "I'll be with you in just a moment."

"No hurry."

The deep, masculine voice fired her heart into her throat as if from a slingshot. She spun around, slamming the drawer shut with her elbow. The *crack!* made her jump, and she felt a blush climbing her cheeks. She twisted her hands together behind her back to keep from covering her face.

"G–good morning." Her voice sounded unnaturally high, unnaturally bright. The heat in her face increased. *Just knock it off, Carrie!*

"Good morning." A lazy smile — the same one that had set her heart to beating like

44

the bass drum in a marching band yesterday — tipped up his lips. His brown eyes sparkled warmly. He wore another T-shirt with the sleeves cut off, and on the right side a string dangled, calling attention to his clearly defined bicep.

She forced her gaze downward to his hand and encountered the wicker basket she'd left outside the tool shed, its napkin crumpled in the bottom. So he'd found the muffins. She swallowed hard and raised her gaze to meet his.

"I–I wondered . . ." Rocky lifted the basket and waved it up and down. "Someone left me a little surprise this morning. Was it you?"

For a split second Carrie considered denying it just to avoid having to explain why she'd done it. But she couldn't make herself lie. She also couldn't find her voice. What was it about this man that made her tongue-tied? She'd never suffered such an intense reaction to anyone. Silently she offered a quick nod. Scurrying across the floor to the desk, she began shifting things, creating stacks, knowing she was only going to have to unstack everything again later.

His smile widened, bringing out crinkly lines around his eyes. The effect was devastating. Her hands stilled as she found an answering smile building on her face.

"Thank you," he said. "They were really good. I shared them with my friend, Eileen. She said they were good, too."

Eileen? Carrie's heart skipped a beat. So he had a girlfriend. Well, that settled that. Then she mentally kicked herself. What on earth was she thinking? "Oh? Well, good." She finally found her voice. It snapped out tartly. "I'm glad you and *Eileen* enjoyed them."

He seemed to falter for a moment, his smile fading. Then he reached out — she held her breath as his hand neared — and placed the basket on the edge of the desk.

"You'll want your basket back. Thanks again, Carrie." He turned to leave.

He'd pushed the door open, had his foot raised to step out when she called, "Wait!"

He turned back slowly, allowing the door to shut. "Yeah?"

"I–I need to say" — she pulled at the collar of her blouse with one finger — "that is, I thank you for the book. And the flowers yesterday." Curiosity got the best of her, and she blurted out, "Where did you find a replacement for *Loyal Traitor*?"

Rocky's grin returned. "Eileen. She has a whole slew of those romance books, so she was willing to part with one. I'm glad I could replace it."

Eileen again. Carrie turned back to the desk. "Yes, well, tell her thank you for me, will you? It was kind of her to give it up."

Rocky nodded slowly. The smile slipped away again at her sharp tone. "I'll do that. See you around, Carrie." He left.

Carrie sank into the chair and covered her face with her hands. She'd been rude. Again. An attack of jealousy had done it. And she had no reason to be jealous — none whatsoever. With a sigh she shook her head, unstacked all the papers she had slung together and tried to put them in order. But she couldn't concentrate.

Releasing a huff of aggravation, she pushed herself from the desk and stomped toward the door. Her conscience pricked sorely, and she wouldn't be able to work until she'd set things straight. She'd have to find Rocky and apologize. Where would he be in the middle of the morning? Then she heard something fire up — a weed eater, maybe? She followed the sound and located Rocky slicing down the growth next to the foundation of Tower Four.

She waited on the sidewalk until he paused, shutting off the machine to lean over and pick up something. As he bent forward, his T-shirt slid up in the back, and a small book in the rear pocket of his jeans caught her attention. A little testament with a green cover, like the ones the Gideons used to hand out in elementary schools.

Rocky read the Bible? He carried it to work with him? Her heart began to thrum as happiness filled her chest. That must mean he was a Christian.

He turned then and found her watching. He ran his fingers through his hair, leaving it in sweat-stiffened spikes. "Hey. Did you need something?" He seemed wary. She couldn't blame him, after the way she'd just acted in the office.

She took two steps forward, nodding. "Yes. To apologize. I'm sorry I got snappy." She didn't offer an explanation.

He didn't ask for one. Just raised one shoulder in a shrug. "It's okay. Apology accepted." His gaze shot past her shoulder, and he raised his hand to wave.

Carrie looked behind her to see an older lady — mid-sixties probably — on the sidewalk across the courtyard. She recognized her as the resident caretaker for a group of men with handicaps.

The lady held up a plastic grocery sack and hollered, "Martin forgot his lunch! I'm taking it to him. Want to meet at noon at my place for some tuna casserole? Pay you back for that muffin."

"Sure!" Rocky called. "See you then!"

Carrie spun back to face Rocky. So that was who he'd shared the muffins with. Then that meant — She fought the urge to giggle as she realized how misplaced her jealousy had been. Eileen was obviously not Rocky's girlfriend. Rocky's attractiveness, the gift of the book and flowers, and the little testament in his back pocket all combined to create a picture Carrie wanted to explore more thoroughly.

"Rocky," she heard herself say, "what are you doing after work?"

He shielded his eyes with his broad hand. "Nothing. Why?"

Surprised by her own audacity, Carrie asked, "I thought maybe we could take a walk around the grounds. Get . . . acquainted."

He seemed to study her for a few silent minutes, and she held her breath, certain he would refuse. But finally he nodded. "Yeah. Okay. That sounds good. Want me to come by the office around four?"

"How about I come looking for you when I'm finished?" She thought of the mess she'd made of the stacks of paperwork on the desk. "I have some catching up to do in the office."

"Okay then."

Her heart tripped happily at the prospect.

He stepped forward, swinging his hand toward her. "Here you go. It's just a weed, but I hated to whack it off when it's so pretty."

Between his fingers he held a fragile green stem with a cup-shaped white flower on its end. Carrie thought her heart might melt. She took the tiny blossom, pressed it to her bodice and gave Rocky the biggest smile she knew how to give. Then she dashed down the sidewalk.

FOUR

Rocky lifted the handle on the hydrant behind the tool shed. The pipe jerked for a few seconds; then water spurted out in a solid flow. He pushed his forearms under the rush and used his hands to scrub away the bits of grass, dust, and sweat all the way from his wrists to his shoulders. The water was ice cold. It made him shiver, but it felt good. Cupping his hands, he trapped water and splashed it over his face once, twice, then again. Finally he ran his wet hands over his hair, smoothing the wild strands into place.

He slammed down the hydrant's handle, stopping the flow, and glanced at his clothes. Too bad he couldn't pop his whole self under that water and really get clean. His jeans showed signs of his labors — dirt smudges, grass stains, and even a blotch of oil from refilling the mower's oil pan. Nothing he could do about that, though. Maybe he should start carting a clean pair of jeans and a shirt to work every day, just in case. . . .

Aw, what was he thinking now? He stomped away from the hydrant and entered the shed to lean against the workbench. It was stuffy in the shed, but he stayed put anyway, out of sight. He felt a strange tremble in his belly that had nothing to do with the shock of cold water after being in the sun all day. The tremble was nervous excitement.

Carrie.

Just her name was enough to make his gut clench. He couldn't quite figure out what made her so special. He'd been around pretty girls before. Been around girls who dressed nice and smelled good, too. But somehow when Carrie dressed nice, it looked natural, not made up. And instead of perfumey, she smelled — he crunched his forehead, trying to identify the scent — like apples. That was it. She always smelled like apples — a clean, fresh scent that suited her clean, fresh appearance.

He chipped at some loose paint on the workbench with his thumbnail as he considered the next hour or so in her company. He pictured them side by side — him in his grubby work clothes, smelling of earth and sweat, her in her green blouse and flowered skirt, smelling of fresh fruit. What a pair they made. Why would she want to spend time with him? He couldn't imagine.

But one thing he knew — he'd enjoy every minute of it. It was doubtful Carrie would ever ask to go for a walk with him again. When would they have the chance? So he'd enjoy today. He sure wished his stomach would settle down though. To calm himself he slipped his New Testament from his back pocket and hunted for words of encouragement.

He felt inept as he flipped random pages, scanning text that was still pretty unfamiliar. But then in the fifteenth chapter of John he latched onto verse sixteen. He read the words aloud. " 'Ye have not chosen me, but I have chosen you, and ordained you, that ye should go and bring forth fruit, and that your fruit should remain: that whatsoever ye shall ask of the Father in my name, he may give it you.' "

Rocky chuckled. "Well, God, that sounds pretty good, considering how Carrie smells like apples and I spent some time transplanting a crab apple tree by the swimming pool this afternoon. And I like the idea of asking for something in Your name and actually getting it. So, if You don't mind, could You give me a calm stomach? Get rid of the nervousness. I'd like to enjoy my time with Carrie, not be afraid of it."

Funny. The prayer did make his stomach feel better. He smiled toward the ceiling. "Thanks a lot, God." As he slipped the Bible back into his pocket, he heard a scuffle. His gaze landed on the doorway, and he found Carrie waiting, a timid smile on her face. He pushed off from the workbench. Had she heard him praying?

He shot past her into the sunshine, a cold sweat breaking out across his shoulders and back. "Hey, Carrie. Ready for that walk?"

She stepped aside as he closed the shed doors and slipped a padlock into place. "Yes. But you'll have to choose where we go. I'm not all that familiar with the grounds. It's been awhile since I was out here on a regular basis."

Rocky heard the quaver in her voice. She must be nervous, too. He found that comforting. Offering a smile, he said, "We've got a nice walking path that leads to the pool, along the golf course and back. It's about a two-mile hike. Are you up to that?"

"Sure."

"Then let's go."

They walked in silence for several minutes, taking slow, relaxed steps. Carrie had some sort of high-heeled sandals with a strap across her toes but no other way to hold the shoe on her foot, and Rocky worried she might fall out of the things. He noticed she moved gracefully, though, despite the dangerous-looking footwear. He swallowed and turned his gaze across the grounds. Pride filled him as he took in the neatly manicured lawns, trimmed shrubs, and garden plots. All the fruits of his labor.

The verse from John — the part about being ordained to bring forth fruit — mingled with Eileen's words, "You've got a knack," and he found himself admitting a real interest in doing this kind of work on his own. Could it be God had that in mind for him, too?

"Things look so nice and neat." Carrie's soft voice intruded into Rocky's thoughts.

"Thanks." He glanced at her, giving her an appreciative smile. "I work pretty hard at it."

"I can tell." She paused beside the spot of ground he'd dug that morning for Eileen's tulips. "I mean, just the shape of this area. It mimics the curve of the sidewalk yet is different enough that it's eye-catching, something an artist would do. Did you get the idea from a gardening book?"

Rocky shoved his hands into his pockets.

"No. I just laid out a garden hose and played with it until I found a shape I liked."

She looked at him, her blue eyes wide. "A garden hose? What an ingenious idea."

Ingenious. She'd said he was ingenious. Rocky thought his chest might explode. He shrugged and forced a calm tone. "Whatever works."

They started walking again, following the concrete path. The sun felt hot on Rocky's head, and he noticed little beads of sweat on Carrie's nose, but she didn't complain. He didn't either. Usually by this time he was plunked in his recliner in front of the little window air conditioning unit in his trailer. But walking in the sunshine with Carrie was even better than sitting under that cold blast of air.

"So . . . all of these garden areas. . . ." She tucked her hair behind her ear and peeked up at him. "Did you design all of them?"

Rocky shook his head. "No, not quite. Eileen and her boys — that's what she calls John, Tim, and Martin, the three men in her quad — started planting flowers last spring. Eileen likes color, and the grounds had bushes but not many flowers. She was spending her own money, buying flowers; then she and her boys would plant them."

He scratched his head, chuckling. That

Eileen was something else. "I told her I'd help, so I started looking for places where the residents might enjoy seeing some flowering plants and also tried to think of the overall appearance of the grounds, giving it a balance of grassy and flowered areas."

"Well, you've done a commendable job. I would imagine the owners are pleased."

"I hope so. They haven't fussed about it anyway."

They passed the swimming pool where two women in one-piece suits and bathing caps stood in waist deep water and visited. Carrie waved when the women waved; then she turned back to Rocky. "How long have you worked here?"

"About eight months. I like it, but —" He stopped his flow of words, aware he nearly let something slip that was a barely formed idea in his mind.

Carrie came to a halt and looked up at him, squinting against the sun. "But?"

Rocky chewed his upper lip. His hand found the testament in his back pocket, and he ran his thumb along the top edge of the book. Carrie's compliments, Eileen's comment, and the verse from John seemed to point him toward accepting the idea as one he should pursue. Yet there were stumbling blocks. Big ones.

Instead of addressing Carrie's question, he asked bluntly, "Are you a Christian?"

Those blue eyes snapped open. She tucked her hair behind her ears and nodded. "Yes. I accepted Christ about a year and a half ago, at a college crusade meeting."

College. Rocky swallowed hard. "Then can I ask you to do something?"

She waited, her expression expectant.

"Would you pray for something? I–I have this idea. A dream, I guess, of what I'd like to do. But it'll be tough. It'll take some minor miracles, I think, to make it happen."

Her soft laughter made him want to smile, too. She held her hands outward in a gesture of inquiry. "Well, what is it?"

Rocky pointed to a bench along the pathway and guided her there. They sat, and eagerness built in his chest as he finally gave voice to his thoughts. "I really like landscaping. Eileen says I have a knack, and — well, I've never been quite sure what I wanted to do with myself." He scratched his head again, somewhat embarrassed. "I guess it's not too good to finally be deciding that when I left high school behind eleven years ago, but. . . ."

Carrie's gaze never wavered from his face. Her genuine interest gave him the confidence to continue.

"But I've been thinking maybe I could open my own landscaping business. Contract myself out to plan the grounds for homes and businesses."

Carrie tipped her head. "Why do you think that will take a minor miracle to make happen?"

Rocky stretched his legs out straight and crossed his ankles. "Well, I'm sure not rolling in dough, if you know what I mean. Schooling takes money."

Carrie seemed to stiffen suddenly, her gaze narrowing.

Rocky went on. "And I'm sure not smart enough to get those scholarships and things some people do — besides that, I'm probably too old to apply. It also takes money to get a business up and running. Advertising, tools, employees. So somehow God's gonna have to come up with the funds. So there's my prayer request. Would you mind praying with me, that if this is what I'm supposed to do God will make the money available?"

Carrie stared hard into Rocky's face. She felt as though a boulder had dropped into her stomach when he'd said he wasn't "rolling in dough." Did he know she was? Did he expect her to offer him the money? She didn't want to think ill of Rocky — his simple prayer in the tool shed had touched her. He'd admitted to being afraid of spending time with her. She had assumed it was nervousness, but now she wondered. Did his fear stem from knowing she had the financial backing to make his dream a reality?

Oh, how she wished she could escape the Steinwood legacy of wealth! She was so tired of second-guessing people's motives. Just once she'd like to relax, to know without any doubt the person wanted to be with her for herself, not for what she could give them.

Rocky sat silently, waiting for her response. She had to say something. "How — how much have you researched this idea?"

He grimaced. "Not a lot, I admit. It's really a new idea. In fact, you're the first person I've even talked to about it."

"Oh, really?" Her heart constricted. Why would he choose her?

"Yeah. Maybe you can help me out some. You must be friends with the owners of Elmwood Towers since you're filling in for the manager. Do you know whether they'd recommend me for other jobs if I started a landscaping business?"

Friends with the owner? Didn't he know

she was the owner's stepdaughter? Or was he playing dumb, hoping to convince her to use some of Mac's money to give him what he wanted? Confusion raced through Carrie's head. She didn't want to play games with Rocky. She wanted him to be honest with her. And she needed to be honest with him, so she took a big breath and confessed, "I guess you could say I'm friends with the owners. Mac Steinwood is my stepfather."

He jerked backward so sharply he nearly fell off the bench. "You're Caroline Steinwood?"

His shock did not seem contrived, but a part of Carrie still wondered. "You honestly didn't know that?"

"No. I mean . . ." He shook his head then ran his hand through his hair. "We never gave our last names. Caroline Steinwood."

"Actually Mays," she corrected. "I go by my father's name. Mac never adopted me." His genuine surprise convinced her he hadn't deliberately set out to use her influence. A sense of relief came with the realization.

"Still . . ." Rocky scooted over a few inches, putting some space between them. His breath huffed out. "Wow, I would've never imagined spending time with Caroline Steinwood."

He sounded impressed. Carrie lowered her head. Now things wouldn't be the same. Dollar signs. All he'd see would be dollar signs from here on out. She stood. "I'd probably better head for home. My folks will be expecting me."

Rocky stood, too. He pushed his hands into his pockets. "Okay. Let's go back to the office then." They continued along the walking path, neither speaking, until they were nearly to the Towers. Suddenly Rocky touched her arm, bringing her to a halt. "Carrie, I really would appreciate it if you'd pray for God to make my idea happen. If it's meant to be, I mean."

She looked into his brown eyes, searching for any sign of insincerity. Maybe it was wishful thinking, but she could see none. She licked her lips and nodded. "I will pray for you, Rocky."

The smile that broke across his face set her heart to thumpity-thumping. "Thank you."

"You're welcome." She stepped away from his warm hand. "Maybe we could meet for lunch tomorrow. I could give you some ideas on classes that would be helpful to a landscaper."

"I *knew* you were the one to ask!" He socked the air, the same way he had the day he'd sprayed her with water. "Sure. Let's have lunch in the courtyard. It's shady there."

Oh, how she hoped she wasn't making a mistake. Before retrieving her purse from the office, she asked, "Rocky, what's your last name?"

"It's Wilder. Rocky Wilder."

Did she imagine it, or did he hesitate? She forced a smile. "Rocky Wilder." She'd heard that name somewhere before. "Okay. Lunch in the courtyard tomorrow. But leave the watering system off, okay?"

He laughed, showing his white teeth. "You got it, Carrie. See you tomorrow." He turned and trotted in the opposite direction across the neatly trimmed grass.

She stood for long moments, watching him, conflicting emotions at war. How her heart wanted to trust him. But her head maintained some doubt. "Lord, don't let me be used again, please," she begged as she finally moved toward the office. "I don't think I could handle it this time."

FIVE

Rocky stopped beside a camellia bush and used his pocket knife to slice through a stem, releasing one red bloom. He'd gotten a glimpse of Carrie through the window this morning, so he knew the flower would match the red and white pantsuit she was wearing.

He whistled as he headed for the office. Each day for the past eight days he'd delivered some sort of flowers to Carrie to put in the little vase she'd brought from home; then they had eaten lunch together in the courtyard. After today Jim would be back, which would bring an end to his daily contact with Carrie. He would miss her. His whistle faded, and he released a sad huff of breath, his shoulders slumping. He would miss her a lot.

But, he reminded himself, picking up his pace, there was still today. One more lunch. One more conversation. That was something to enjoy. He opened the door to the office and stepped through. "Hey, ready for lunch?"

Carrie rose from the desk with a smile, holding out her hand to take the blossom he offered. "Yes, I am. And thank you for the flower. It's lovely." She rolled the stem of the camellia between her fingers while she talked. "I brought some brownies today. They have white chocolate chunks and macadamia nuts in them, and Myrna says they're famous at her son's school."

"That sounds great," he said.

She leaned toward the vase, ready to place the camellia with yesterday's Michaelmas daisies.

"Wait!" He took the bloom back and stepped beside her. "Here." She'd pulled her hair into a sleek ponytail, held with a silver barrette at the base of her skull. He carefully slipped the stem of the flower into the hair behind her left ear then moved back and smiled. "Yes, that's perfect." The flower sat directly above her ear, bringing out the sparkle of her blue eyes. "Although I have to say, as pretty as that flower is, it pales when compared to you."

To his delight a blush stole across her cheeks. "Rocky, really, you are such a flatterer."

"Hey, whatever works," he quipped with a grin. Then he shrugged. "I heard some movie hero say that to his girl, and I've waited for the right girl to repeat it to."

Her blush deepened, and she pointed to the door. "Let's go get started on lunch, huh?" She gave his shoulder a playful push, and they headed for their bench.

Once settled, Rocky said grace, feeling a little nervous about praying out loud in front of Carrie, yet good, too. They ate their sandwiches — Carrie had her favorite, tuna salad with raw spinach, and Rocky had his typical bologna and American cheese — and they shared the brownies, all the while chatting easily about anything that came to mind.

When Rocky finished the last bite of brownie, he let out a sigh of pleasure and admitted, "I'm gonna miss seeing you every day, you know? You've become a pretty good friend, for a girl."

Carrie laughed. "Well, I'm not sure whether I should be insulted by that or not."

He grinned. "You know what I mean. Doesn't happen too often that guys and girls become friends. Usually you start talking to a girl, and she either decides she doesn't like you and runs in the opposite direction, or she decides she likes you too much and runs after you. It's kind of nice just to ease into things, you know? Comfortable."

Carrie nodded, her expression thoughtful. "I suppose I hadn't thought of it that way, but you're right. It has been comfortable. I've enjoyed getting to know you, too."

"So." His lips suddenly felt dry, and he rubbed them together as he gathered his courage. "What do we do now? I mean, obviously you won't be back since Jim's vacation is over. But — can we maybe still continue the friendship? See each other away from Elmwood Towers?" He thought his heart might pound right out of his chest while he waited for her to answer.

"Well . . ." She looked across the courtyard, as if deep in thought. "I'll be back in school again in another few days. My course schedule is pretty taxing, Rocky, and my days are full."

She was letting him down. His chest felt tight. She'd had her summer fling, but now it was over. He steeled himself for the rejection.

"But weekends? I work hard during the week to keep my weekends free. Maybe we could get together on a Friday or Saturday evening sometime."

He tried not to sound too eager. "That

would be great."

She turned a smile in his direction. "I think so, too. How about a week from today? That will be my first Friday evening after starting classes. I'll be ready for a break."

He supposed he could last a week without seeing her. "Okay, sure." Suddenly he scowled. "By the way, Carrie, what are you working toward — in college, I mean? You don't talk much about yourself."

"I have a degree in business administration and am working toward one in computer programming." Her nonchalant tone nearly cut Rocky to the quick. "It will take me another year, probably, to finish everything up, but it will qualify me for many executive positions. My parents strongly encouraged me to be marketable."

Did he hear some resentment in her tone? He couldn't be sure. But he knew this — her words made him feel inadequate. Business administration. Computer programming. Executive position. Marketable. And here he sat, with his biggest dream being able to plunk plants in the ground for the rest of his life. He shouldn't even be sitting on this bench with her, let alone pursuing a relationship beyond the confines of Elmwood Towers. Who did he think he was?

Carrie watched Rocky's demeanor change. He'd been attentive and open only a moment ago, but now he closed off. She saw his withdrawal in the way he pulled his arms inward, pressing his palms together and forcing them between his knees. She hoped he wasn't upset that she wouldn't be available every day. As much as she had enjoyed meeting him for lunch and chatting each day, she had to be honest with him — her college course work took up most of her week. Spending time with him on weekends seemed ideal to her, but it didn't seem to please him. How she hoped he wouldn't turn possessive now. She simply did not have the energy to deal with that and concentrate on her studies.

She glanced at her wristwatch. "I guess it's almost one, isn't it? I'd better get back to the office. I want to make sure everything is well organized so Jim won't have any question about what I did in his absence."

Rocky stood, crumpling his lunch sack. "I've got things to do, too. Eileen and I are going to bury her tulip bulbs this afternoon when the boys return." But his voice lacked the usual enthusiasm.

Carrie swallowed hard. "Well, then — will I see you next Friday?"

"You really want to?"

She shook her head, smiling. "Rocky, I wouldn't ask if I didn't want to." The safest course, to stave off any possessiveness, would be to keep things casual. Before he could ask if he should pick her up, she suggested, "There's a pizza place — the Ironstone — on the corner of Main and Baker Avenue. Should we meet there at seven? We can share a stone-baked pizza and a pitcher of pop."

He offered a slow nod, and his lips tugged into a smile although his eyes remained dim. "Sure, Carrie. That sounds good."

What should they do now? Shake hands? Hug? Carrie found herself floundering. The one thing she hadn't felt around Rocky was awkward; yet the moment was rife with discomfort as they tried to say good-bye. Finally, in Rocky's silence, Carrie just blurted out, "Well, I'll see you in a week then. 'Bye, Rocky."

His good-bye came out softly, tinged with a regret she didn't understand. It echoed in her mind the remainder of the afternoon and tormented her on the drive home. Men! Would she ever understand them? Once home she headed to her bedroom and removed the camellia from her hair. She laid the flower on her bedside table, changed into a pair of khaki shorts and a silk tank top then flopped across her bed with her telephone in her hand. If anyone could help her make sense of Rocky's behavior, it would be Angela Fisher.

Angela was the most well-dated friend in Carrie's circle. She openly admitted she enjoyed the company of men, and she flitted from one to another without ever making a serious commitment. Sometimes Carrie thought Angela was an airhead, and she certainly disapproved of some of her choices, but in this case perhaps Angela could offer some advice on how to proceed with Rocky.

Angela answered her phone on the second ring with a chirpy "Hello!"

"Hi, Angela. This is Carrie."

"Carrie!" The word nearly squealed out. "Does this mean you're done with that job? Are you free tonight? We're having a major gathering at my pool house — an end-of-summer bash. Want to join us?"

Carrie rolled to her back. "Probably not, although I appreciate the invitation. I've got some things to catch up on here at home since school is just around the corner."

"Oh, girl, you're too serious." Angela's

chiding voice carried clearly through the lines. Carrie could picture the other girl's face pinched in displeasure.

"Besides," Carrie inserted gently, "your parties always seem to include alcohol, and I'm not comfortable with that."

"As I said, *too* serious." Angela never took anything seriously. "Okay. Don't come. There will be plenty of action without you. So . . . what did you need?"

"Actually, some advice." Carrie suddenly wondered at the sense of asking advice from Angela. Her opinion would surely be tainted by her own lack of Christian morals. Yet she wasn't sure who else would have the experience Angela did when it came to dating. She proceeded cautiously. "You see, I've gotten acquainted with someone the past couple of weeks."

"Ooooh, do tell!"

Carrie cringed at the undertone. "It's nothing like that." She stroked the petals of the camellia with her finger. "Just a friendship, really, but I'm not sure whether I should continue it."

"So what does he do for a living?"

Of course. The roundabout way of finding out if he was rich. Carrie sucked in her breath. "He's a gardener." The laughter at the other end of the phone made Carrie mad. "Quit it, Angela. He's a really nice guy."

"Okay, okay, sorry." The laughter stopped, but humor was still evident in her voice. "Does this *gardener* have a name?"

Carrie considered hanging up, but she forged onward. "Yes, he does. It's Rocky Wilder."

There was a shocked silence, followed by an explosion. "Rocky Wilder! Carrie, you have got to be kidding!"

Carrie frowned. What was that all about? "No, I'm not kidding. Why do you say it like that?"

"Carrie, Rocky Wilder was in my sister Audrey's class in school." Angela babbled so fast Carrie had a hard time catching all the words. "He was a *mess* with a capital *M!* Always creating a ruckus, picking on people, stealing things, arguing with teachers. He set the record for in-school suspensions. Honestly, Audrey was scared to death of him! He got into some real serious trouble when he was, like, thirteen or fourteen and even got sent to reform school for awhile.

"Rocky Wilder is *trouble,* Carrie. Don't even think about a friendship with him! He'll rob you blind, and I'm not just talkin' money. I'm talking about your heart, honey.

He'll use it, abuse it, and leave you high and dry. Run — don't walk — run away as fast and as far as you can from that man! You'll be much better off, believe me."

Carrie sat in stunned silence. The person Angela just described couldn't possibly be the same man with whom she'd spent the last two weeks. She managed a weak thank-you then hung up, reeling. Staring at the ceiling, she envisioned Rocky as she'd seen him once earlier this week. He hadn't even been aware of her presence, because he'd been reading the New Testament he carried in his pocket. The look on his face as he'd read the Bible — he'd been so engrossed, it almost seemed as though he were absorbing the words. She hadn't had the heart to bother him, so she'd crept away.

The man she'd seen soaking up God's Word couldn't be anything like the one Angela had depicted . . . could he? If Angela was right, if Rocky truly was someone who'd been consistently in trouble, then he certainly had learned how to play games. He could deceive her. Suddenly she felt queasy. She really didn't want to believe it, but doubts pressed in.

How many other men had duped her in the past, complimenting her, pursuing her . . . and doing it only because she had money. Rocky didn't have money — he'd openly admitted that. Did he see her as his opportunity for wealth? Would he use her and abuse her, as Angela had said? Or could she trust him?

She groaned, pressing her face against her pillow shams. "Dear Lord, please help me sort this out. What is the truth?" She prayed for several minutes, pouring out her frustration and worries to her heavenly Father. The prayer finished, she had no clear answers, but she felt calmer.

Slipping from the bed, she crossed to the window and looked down at her mother's rose garden in the backyard. Their gardener took as much pride in his work as Rocky did in his. How fortunate both men were, Carrie decided, to be able to see so clearly the results of their labor. How wonderful to create something of such beauty. She propped her chin on her hand, catching her elbow with her other hand, and stared pensively down at the profusion of color.

The man Angela described would not be capable of creating beauty. Angela had spoken of a man who created chaos. She supposed Rocky was creating chaos in her heart, but she wasn't quite ready to believe he would create chaos in every other aspect of her life. She needed to explore his person more deeply — develop their friendship and allow it to bloom as fully as one of the prize roses in Mother's garden. Once the bloom was open, she'd be able to see Rocky for who he truly was.

But to see that open bloom she would need time with him. She turned from the window and picked up the camellia blossom again. It was wilted and sad-looking now, but the color was still deep and rich. She cradled the flower gently in her palm as she made her decision.

She would meet Rocky next Friday. And she would ask the kinds of questions that would help her see his true character. In the meantime, she'd pray for God to open her eyes to the truth, whatever that might be.

Six

The Monday following the manager's return, Rocky went to the familiar bench in the center of the courtyard to eat his lunch, but it didn't feel right without Carrie. His sandwich tasted like cardboard. Dissatisfaction filled his middle, making it hard to swallow. Plunking the sandwich back into its baggy, he blew out a frustrated breath. Who would have thought Rocky Wilder, toughest kid on the block, would be struck down by puppy love?

Yet it was true. He couldn't get Carrie off his mind. And he needed to. The relationship couldn't go anywhere. He'd suspected they were different when he'd first seen her in her cute little beaded outfit with a soggy sandwich in her manicured hand. But when she'd said she was a Steinwood — that pretty much settled it. They were worlds apart.

He recalled his embarrassment when

she'd told him about the degree she was working toward in college. Carrie had to be smart to handle all that. One degree in business administration and another in computer programming. He shook his head, trying to comprehend all that would entail.

Rocky had used computers in high school, but he didn't own one — he couldn't afford it. And business administration — his brother, Philip, ran his own business, but Philip had the brains in the Wilder family. He was fooling himself, thinking he could handle running his own landscaping business. He wasn't smart like Philip and Carrie. He didn't have money like Carrie, to hire someone to help him. If, as he suspected, he was falling in love with Carrie, he'd want to take care of her and the children they might have together. How would he be able to do that on a gardener's salary? He couldn't. It wasn't possible.

He groaned, leaning forward and resting his elbows on his knees, dejection striking. A part of him could hardly wait until Friday arrived, when he'd be able to see her again, and a part of him dreaded Friday, when he'd have to see her again and be reminded of just how impossible continuing a friendship would be.

He felt so lonely out there on the bench

by himself.

"Rocky!"

The voice jerked him out of his reverie. He looked over his shoulder and spotted Eileen standing in the open doorway of Tower Three.

She waved her arm at him. "Come upstairs and have lunch with me! And you can call Philip on my phone."

Rocky balled up what was left of his lunch as he trotted to Eileen. Pitching his lunch in the trash can next to the entrance to Tower Three, he said, "Sounds great! But call Philip? Why?" Eileen shook her gray head as she led him to the elevator. "No emergency. He just said he needed to talk to you about something going on at church, and he couldn't reach you at home. Says you need to get a cell phone."

Rocky nearly laughed out loud at that. A cell phone? Those things were for preppy teenagers or business execs, not a man on a gardener's salary. Carrie probably had one, though. He pushed that thought away as he followed Eileen out of the elevator to her apartment. A tantalizing smell greeted his nostrils as she opened the door, and his stomach rolled over in eagerness. He stepped past a sleeping Roscoe, who lay on his back in the middle of the walkway with his front paws curled beneath his furry chin.

"Boy, I sure appreciate this invitation." Rocky sat at the bar and let Eileen serve him a steaming bowl of noodles swimming in a thick broth with chunks of chicken and topped by two plump dumplings.

"I appreciate the company," she told him. "Pray and eat."

He followed her direction, and when he'd finished he used Eileen's telephone to give his brother a quick call. "Hey, Philip, what's going on?"

"Oh, good, Eileen found you. Listen — there's a Bible study starting at church this Wednesday I think you would enjoy. I took the class a year or so ago, and I really gained a lot from it."

Rocky twisted his face into an uncertain scowl. "Bible study? I don't know." He thought about Sunday mornings and the length of time it took him to find references as the preacher spoke. He felt stupid when he couldn't locate things quickly. And a Bible study would be held in a smaller group. His groping would be more noticeable.

"It's a good one," Philip's voice went on, "on the Fatherhood of God. It helped me come to terms with my earthly father. Our dad wasn't all bad, but he wasn't the best influence. This study helped me settle into my place in God's family. I think you'd get a lot out of it, Rocky."

Rocky scratched his head. "Well . . . Wednesday, you said?"

"Yes. In the church basement." A light chuckle came through the line. "They serve refreshments with it, if that sweetens the pot."

Rocky laughed. "Great motivator. I'll think about it, okay?" He hung up and joined Eileen at the kitchen sink where she washed their few dishes.

"Philip told me about a Bible study he thinks would be good for me," he told her as he picked up a dish towel and dried a bowl. "Something about the Fatherhood of God."

Eileen swished her hand through the water then rubbed the soapy rag over the spoon she located. "Bible study's always good for people."

"Yeah, but" — he opened a cupboard to put away the dry bowl — "I always feel lost scrambling around for verses. Maybe I should wait until I know my way around the Bible better."

Eileen gave him one of her famous eyebrows-high-chin-tucked-low looks. "That's just silly. How do you get familiar with something? You use it regularly. How'd you get so good at that landscaping out there? By standing on the sidelines? Nope, had to dive in and do it. Same thing applies to that Bible of yours. Might as well be practicing getting around while you're learning something at the same time, right? Go to the study, Rocky."

Rocky shook his head, chuckling. "You never mince words, do you?"

She shrugged and handed him the last of the silverware. "Too old to be mincing words. So are you going or not?"

"We'll see," he said, unwilling to commit just yet. The dishes done, he thanked Eileen for the lunch and the use of her phone, took a few moments to scratch Roscoe's neck then headed back to work.

The Bible study and the idea of looking at God as his Father teased Rocky's thoughts for the next two days. His earthly father hadn't been the easiest man to live with, and truthfully Rocky wasn't sure he liked the idea of applying the term "Father" to God. He'd rather keep his ideas of father and God separate. Yet when Wednesday rolled around, the opportunity to gain a better understanding of his relationship with God found him climbing into his old clunker and driving to church.

Roughly twenty people were already in the basement when Rocky arrived, and relief washed over him when he saw they were casually dressed. He wouldn't stick out in his clean dungarees and snap-up Western-style shirt. He helped himself to three vanilla cream-filled cookies and a cup of tea then sat on the outside aisle of the second row. He ate his snack while waiting for things to get started.

At seven o'clock on the dot, the teacher — a mid-thirties man with a receding hairline and thick glasses — stepped behind the podium and had them go around the room and introduce themselves. Rocky's hand trembled as he stated his name. He never knew whether someone would recognize him as that messed up Wilder boy, and he was relieved when the attention moved on to the person seated behind him.

Once the introductions were over, the teacher instructed everyone to open their Bibles to the book of Galatians, chapter four, starting with verse six. Rocky found the reference in time to hear the last few words of verse seven: "God has made you also an heir." He slipped a pen from his pocket and made a note in the margin to remind him to go back and read the section again later.

As the evening wore on, he forgot his discomfort about not being able to locate things quickly and got caught up in the lesson. His heart pounded with eagerness to accept not only that Jesus was his Savior but that God was his Father. He, Rocky Wilder, could take his place as one of God's heirs. To think God loved him enough to adopt him into His family.

A feeling of acceptance, the likes of which Rocky had never before experienced, filled him and brought tears to his eyes. He swallowed hard to bring himself under control then fixed his gaze on the teacher and listened with his whole heart.

Carrie was disappointed she'd missed the first part of the Bible study. Frustration with her stepfather still sat like a weight on her chest as she slipped in quietly and took the least obtrusive open seat, in the middle of the last row.

She settled in the chair and peeked at the Bible in the lap of the person on her left. Flipping open her own Bible to the same place, her thoughts raged on. Why couldn't Mac just let her go to church without creating a scene? Her church attendance took nothing away from him; yet he opposed it as adamantly as if she were attending a meeting to overthrow the government. Right now she needed to lean into the idea that God was her Father. How she hoped her Father in heaven would help her deal patiently and kindly with the father she had on earth!

She tried to focus on what the teacher was saying, but her thoughts were still too jumbled from the confrontation at home. Mac insisted she needed to give her whole attention to college and job-seeking, that anything outside of that created a diversion which might ruin any future opportunity for success. Church attendance ruin her opportunity for success? That made no sense to Carrie. Mac was completely unreasonable.

Mac's ranting had certainly created a diversion from gaining anything from this study! She had to get focused here. To settle herself in, she allowed her gaze to drift across the rows one by one, seeing how many people she knew. After attending this church for a little over a year, she'd gotten acquainted with a handful of college-age students, but most of these people weren't from her Sunday school class.

Her gaze reached the second row from the front, and she had to tip her head slightly to see all the way to the end. When she found the familiar thick head of sun-bleached dark hair belonging to Rocky Wilder, her heart jumped into her throat and lodged.

Angela's words echoed in her mind: *Run — don't walk — run away as fast and as far as you can from that man!* Almost of its own volition her body recoiled, pressing against the cold back of the metal folding chair in an attempt to shield herself from his view. Her pulse raced — how did he know she would be here this evening? Then she made herself calm down. She hadn't even known she would be here until earlier in the day when one of her Sunday school classmates had called. There was no way Rocky could have known. It was a coincidence. Angela's ominous words were making her paranoid.

Get a grip, Carrie, she told herself firmly. *Rocky's no stalker.* In fact, as she watched him, it became clear he was unaware of anything in the room except what the speaker was saying. His gaze bounced from the teacher to his Bible — a full-sized one, not the little testament he carried to work. His fingers raced to find the scriptures mentioned. A napkin holding a half-eaten cookie rested on his knee, but he ignored it, his attention obviously on gaining spiritual food.

Something warm and soothing spiraled

through Carrie's middle. She relaxed in the chair, a smile found itself forming on her lips, and a silent prayer went up from her heart. *Thank You, God, for giving me this glimpse of Rocky. He's no longer that man Angela described; he is a new creature in You. I can see it.*

She turned her attention to the teacher. It was nearly seven thirty, the class half over. She'd better pay attention to what remained. At the close of class the teacher asked for prayer requests. Several people voiced concerns, which the teacher wrote on a white board behind his podium. Carrie waited for Rocky to ask for prayer for his new business venture, but he remained silent. She considered asking for him, but she decided that would be breaking a confidence. Instead, as the teacher prayed, she prayed, too, asking that if Rocky's dream was God's will, it might become a reality.

People rose to leave, and Carrie slipped her purse over her shoulder, intending to catch Rocky and talk to him. But someone grasped her arm and turned her around.

"Carl!" What was he doing here? Although it had been months since she'd seen him, the reaction to his presence was intense. Her heart picked up its tempo, she felt a prickle of awareness tingle down her spine, and she fought an urge to dash away.

"Hi, Carrie." His thumb caressed the bare skin of her upper arm. "Mac told me I'd find you here. I've been waiting outside the door for class to finish."

She pulled her arm free. "Why?" She tried not to sound snappish, but her jangled nerves made the word come out more harshly than she intended.

He ducked his head, bringing professionally added blond highlights to view. "I hoped we could talk."

"What about?"

He glanced around, his expression solemn. "It's kind of personal, Carrie."

She hesitated. As much as she hated to admit it, his grave countenance stirred her sympathy.

"Please?"

The sincerity in his tone did her in. "All right. But give me a minute, will you?" She glanced around, seeking Rocky. She finally located him, but before she could call out he moved through the doorway leading to the stairs. She sighed.

"Everything okay?" Carl asked.

"I wanted to talk to someone, but it's too late now." She turned toward the doors. "Come on then."

He put his hand on the small of her back

and escorted her to the stairway. She bounced up the steps, managing to elude his touch until they reached the foyer, but then his hand was back, warm and firm and possessive. She didn't like it.

He guided her to her car then braced his hand on the roof, leaning in too close for comfort. "I appreciate your doing this for me, Carrie. You're a real doll, you know that?"

Oh yes, she was a real doll, she thought disparagingly, taking a step back to put some distance between the two of them. More likely she was just a sucker who would later regret this time with Carl. She didn't respond.

"Where can we go?"

Carrie considered his question. She didn't want to be seen in public with him. If any of their mutual friends saw them together, tongues would start wagging. She didn't want to go to his townhouse — that would give him the wrong ideas. There was only one alternative.

"Why don't you just follow me to the house? It's a pleasant evening. We can sit on the porch and talk there." She waited for him to move aside so she could get in her car. To her chagrin, when he removed his hand from the roof, he reached out and

89

cupped her cheek, his fingers gracing the line of her jaw.

"Thank you, sweet thing. I really appreciate it."

The nickname he'd given her struck like a blow. Instead of bringing a rush of affection, it brought a jolt of revulsion. She turned her face from his touch. Swallowing the nausea that threatened, she said in a tight voice, "Let's just get going, huh, Carl?"

He smiled, his teeth even and white in the dusky evening light. He opened the door for her. "Okay. I'll follow you to your place. Thanks again."

She nodded. To her relief he pushed off from the car and strode away, his shoulders back and chin high in the familiar pose she'd once thought spoke of confident strength. Now its arrogance turned her stomach. With a sigh she slipped behind the wheel of her car and started the engine. "Let's just get this over with."

SEVEN

Rocky drove toward home, his right arm stretched straight out with his hand gripping the top of the steering wheel, the other arm propped on the window frame — a pose he'd perfected in high school to look cool. But right now he wasn't thinking about looking cool. He was lost in thought.

Wind rushed past his ear, tossing his hair and making his eyes water. He squinted, battling mixed emotions. Part of him celebrated the knowledge he'd gained this evening — God saw him as His adopted son. That realization made his heart sing. Then there was the other part — the heart-crushing part.

Seeing Carrie with that other man.

His fingers tightened on the steering wheel, the image taunting him. The man's thumb slipping up and down on Carrie's skin, the gesture familiar, intimate. Carrie's face turned up to his. Both of them in their designer clothes and styled hair and un-scuffed shoes. They fit together. His heart clenched. They matched.

Once again the differences between Carrie's world and his own struck hard. Just who did he think he was? Maybe he needed a reminder. He glanced at street signs and realized he wasn't too far from his old neighborhood. Slapping the directional signal, he made a left hand turn and wove his way to Avenue D.

Familiar landmarks — the Tasti-Freeze, a weed-infested ball diamond, and a boarded-up warehouse — brought a rush of childhood memories. Turning north on Avenue D, he slowed to a crawl and stared through the gloomy dusk at sad-looking houses, their unkempt lawns littered with bicycles, broken toys, and empty beer cans. Pulling to the curb in front of 1713 Avenue D, he popped the gear shift into neutral and sat, his fingers cupping his chin, and let his gaze slowly sweep across the house where he'd grown up.

Nothing fancy, that was for sure. A post-WWII bungalow — square, the front door centered between two windows. The window on the left was the living room, the window on the right his parents' bedroom. He and Philip had shared the second bedroom which was behind his parents'. He wondered if the same faded cowboys and Indians wallpaper hung on the walls of that room. No way to tell, without going in, and he wouldn't ask to do that. He had no desire to go inside that house again.

He took in the sagging shutters, torn window screens, and peeling paint. It didn't look as if anyone had tried to make improvements since his parents' deaths. Of course, there wasn't much to improve on, Rocky acknowledged. No porch softened the appearance of the house, only a cracked concrete slab with one sloping concrete step. Not even a railing. His mother had tried to plant flowers around the base of the porch, but he and Philip always jumped off the sides and trampled any living thing, preventing the plants from blooming. How Mom hollered at them for that.

And Dad did more than holler. . . .

Rocky sighed. Not many happy memories in that house. He glanced up and down the block, which was nearly hidden in shadow already. A few lights glowed behind window shades. He wondered if any happy childhoods were being played out in other houses around him. He hoped so.

It had seemed to him, as a child and rebellious teen, that happiness only existed in the homes six blocks over — in the neighborhoods with names like Morning Glory Circle and East Briar Estates. Homes with neat lawns and swimming pools and spindled porches where swings or wicker furniture invited a person to sit, relax, and bask in all he owned. On impulse Rocky shifted to drive and made a U-turn, angling his vehicle toward the "rich district."

He crept out of the neighborhood as slowly as he had entered, almost with reverence, offering a prayer for the occupants of each house as he passed by. The houses slowly changed shape and appearance as he rolled along, from small disheveled dwellings to small neater dwellings then to large neater dwellings until he reached the large, ostentatious neighborhood of East Briar Estates.

He felt like an interloper as he guided his old car between the brick pillars standing sentry on either side of the opening to the elite housing district. Homes protected by iron fences, many of them with gates blocking the curving driveways, stood in stark contrast to the neighborhood he'd left behind.

Making a right-hand turn at the first opportunity, he drove slowly past the stately Tudor home where Mac Steinwood and his family lived. How many times, as a boy, had he driven over here on his bicycle and stood outside the iron fence, peering in, wondering what was inside that house? The Steinwood mansion had been his dream house — tall, rambling, surely full of all the things his own family couldn't afford.

If Rocky closed his eyes, he could imagine the shining chandeliers and polished woodwork and — he allowed himself to release a rueful chuckle — a wood-paneled den with a pool table bigger than a king-sized bed. Funny the things that had seemed important back then. . . .

He passed the Steinwood house and cruised around the block, aware of bright lights not only inside but outside each house, like hundreds of eyes watching, protecting. The feeling of being an intruder increased with every change of his odometer. His gaze drifted from the homes themselves to the beautifully landscaped yards. Probably the owners of those houses each had a crew to keep their yards nice — gardeners, like him, paid to bring beauty to the owners' surroundings.

He bet those gardeners never got inside the house, though. Someone who dug in the dirt sure wouldn't be good enough to step through the front door. He clenched his jaw and swallowed. He didn't belong here, and he'd better leave before someone called the cops on him.

One more swing past the Steinwood Estate for old-times' sake; then he'd go home. He paused at the intersection, prepared to turn toward the Steinwoods' when headlights appeared on his right. He waited, and when the car passed him he realized it was Carrie's sports car. She was home from church. His heart pounded as he watched her go by, and it was all he could do to keep from blaring his horn to let her know he was there. But the sight of a second car — a fairly new sports utility vehicle — right behind hers stopped him. The driver was the man he'd seen with Carrie at church.

He held his breath, watching Carrie stop outside the gates for a moment to punch buttons in the box beside the drive. The gates opened, she drove through, and the utility vehicle followed.

Rocky felt sick. The man obviously meant something to Carrie. The man obviously matched Carrie in wealth and education. As it had before, the realization at how well they matched struck like a blow. It was just as well he'd seen them together. It made things clear. He did not belong with Carrie. He did not belong in her world.

Turning his car in the opposite direction, he gunned his motor and raced out of the neighborhood. "So long, Carrie," he shouted out the open window. From here on out, he'd leave her alone.

Carrie stepped out of the garage and met Carl in the driveway. She didn't want to take him in the house where Mac would see them together and make assumptions, so she pointed to the gazebo in the backyard. It was well lit, thanks to the solar lanterns that hung in evenly spaced intervals around the cedar-shingled roof. "Let's sit out here."

Carl followed her without a word across softly illuminated stepping stones, and he waited until she seated herself in one of the cushioned bamboo-framed chairs before choosing the chair directly opposite her. He shot her a practiced smile and said, "This is perfect. You're absolutely breathtaking in the moonlight."

"Stop it, Carl." She frowned to let him know she meant it. "Flattery won't work anymore. You said you needed to talk, so go ahead. I'm listening."

He leaned back, crossed his leg and let out a huff of laughter. "You're in a sour mood."

His cajoling tone did nothing to soften

her. "I'm not in a sour mood. I just don't have time for your insincere compliments."

His posture didn't change an inch nor did his tone. "Insincere compliments? You think I'm insincere?"

"I think you say what you believe will benefit you the most." She pressed into the cushioned back of the chair, bracing her hands on the armrests. "And I'm not the same naïve girl you duped two years ago. So let's just skip the flattery and get to the point."

A night bird sang a lonesome chorus while Carl sat in silence and examined Carrie. She kept a stern pose, her face turned in his direction, and offered no more encouragement. At long last he blew out his breath, raised his hands in a gesture of defeat and said, "Okay. I'll lay it out. I've missed you desperately. I realize I love you." He leaned forward, his voice dropping to a sultry whisper. "I want you back."

Carrie gave an unladylike *hmph.* "Yes, I'll bet you do." She shook her head, the slight breeze tossing one strand of hair across her cheek. She anchored it behind her ear. "But it isn't me you really want, is it, Carl?"

He scowled. "Of course it is. What are you talking about?"

"Come off it. I know you investigated my

trust fund. I know you know, to the penny, exactly what I'm worth. And I know you know I'll be given control of that money in another month, when I turn twenty-five."

His eyebrows shot upward in well-feigned surprise. "Really?" He settled himself back into the chair. "Your birthday is around the corner? Oh, it is! I'd forgotten."

Carrie rolled her eyes. "Please, don't patronize me. I haven't seen or heard from you in almost two years, you show up conveniently just before I'm ready to have a large sum of money at my disposal, and you want me to believe you love me and want me back." She shook her head, her gaze never wavering from his. "What you love is the idea of gaining access to my father's wealth. It's not me. It never was."

Carl stroked his lower lip with his finger while he stared at her, unblinking. "You underestimate yourself, Carrie. Don't you see yourself as lovable without your money?"

She refused to be sidetracked by his glib tongue. "It's not a matter of what *I* see; it's a matter of what *you* see. And when you look at me, you see dollar signs."

He laughed out loud at her, stirring her ire. "Sweet thing, you really are too cute for words. Dollar signs." He continued to chuckle.

"Cute, ugly, it wouldn't matter, as long as I come with the fortune." Carrie ignored his amusement. "And I want something more than a relationship built on a pile of bank notes."

Carl stopped chuckling and leaned forward, his expression fervent. "Tell me what you want, Carrie. Whatever it is, I'll give it to you. Tell me how to prove that I love you."

How could she have ever seen him as handsome? His perfectly placed features were physically appealing, but the hunger in his eyes for material things made him seem so shallow. She berated herself for having given him a piece of her heart. She whispered a silent prayer of thanks for learning the truth before she'd accepted his marriage proposal.

"Carl, there's no way you can prove that to me. And I don't want you to try. It would be demeaning."

"I'd demean myself for you, Carrie. Just say the word."

"Stop it!" He was embarrassing her, and he was embarrassing himself. All for money. It was all so pointless and . . . *sad.* She took a deep breath. "This whole conversation is ridiculous. We have nothing in common, except the fact we both happened to be born to wealthy families. Beyond that" — she lifted her shoulders in a shrug — "there's nothing."

"Define nothing," he shot back.

She had no difficulty with that. "First, and most important, there's faith. I believe Jesus Christ is the Son of God, sent to the world to save us from our sins. I've accepted His gift of salvation. You haven't."

"Tell me how. If that's what you want, I'll do it right now."

His flippant reply made her heart ache for his lack of understanding. "That isn't something you do for someone else. It's something you do for yourself. And it's a commitment, Carl, not a statement you make to impress someone."

He nodded his head slowly. "Okay. Then go on. What else do we not have in common?"

Now she floundered. On many levels she and Carl were compatible, which was why he'd managed to win her before. They had similar backgrounds, similar interests, similar tastes. But she'd found a personal relationship with Jesus since she and Carl had broken up, and she knew none of their similarities would be enough without the common foundation of faith in Christ. Uncertain how to explain herself, she remained silent.

Carl took her silence as an opportunity. Reaching out, he caught her hand, his thumb painting lazy circles on the back of her wrist. "See? There's only that one thing. It could work, Carrie. Give me a chance."

She snatched her hand free and rose. "No, it wouldn't work. That 'one thing,' as you put it, is everything. Without that we have nothing. So there's no point in continuing this discussion. If that's all you wanted, then —"

"Please, Carrie. Don't turn me away." He stood and captured her shoulders with his smooth, tapered fingers. "You still care for me. You aren't dating anyone else."

"Yes, I am." Her adamant contradiction surprised Carl no more than it surprised her. Was she dating Rocky? Not really, yet she knew she wanted to. She stepped backward, freeing herself from his grasp, and darted behind her chair. Feeling safe with the barrier between them, she said boldly, "So this conversation needs to end immediately."

Carl's gaze narrowed as he examined her. "Are you lying to me to get me to back off?"

"I'm not lying. I met someone recently, and we are seeing each other." A picture of Rocky, his head bent over his Bible, his forehead creased in concentration, brought a smile to her lips.

Carl must have seen it, because his expression hardened. "Okay. Fine. I concede defeat." He started for the opening of the gazebo then stopped and turned back, his hand braced on a spindled beam. "But what makes you so sure this guy is any different from how you see me? What makes you so sure he's not after your money, too?"

Carrie felt heat fill her face. She found no words.

He gave a knowing nod. "That's what I thought. Well — be careful, Carrie. You can't separate the girl from the money, you know." He turned and strode away. In moments the engine to his vehicle revved, and he backed out of the drive.

Carrie sank back into the chair, staring into the dark. As much as she hated to admit it, Carl's words had found their mark. Once again the old doubts surfaced. Rocky wasn't wealthy. What if he truly did see her as an end to his financial needs?

"Carrie?"

She glanced up. Her mother stood on the walkway. How long had she been out here? "Hi, Mom."

Her mother entered the gazebo and sat down where Carl had been. "Carl left in a hurry. Is everything okay?"

Briefly Carrie recounted their conversation. She ended with, "Mom, I don't trust Carl, but I do trust Rocky. I know you and Mac think Carl and I would be ideal together, but —" She shook her head, unable to proceed.

"Honey, I know Mac can be pushy, but underneath he only wants what's best for you, as do I." Her mother tipped her head, her silver earrings glinting in the soft light cast by the lanterns. "How well do you know this . . . Rocky?"

Carrie grimaced at the way her mother said Rocky's name. "Not all that well, yet. But I want to get to know him better. He has a gentle strength that I admire, and even though he's a new Christian he's growing. I can see it."

A soft smile graced her mother's face. "You're smitten."

Carrie released a light laugh. "Yes, I suppose I am."

"Well, honey, I suppose you've heard that old adage that opposites attract. But the adage doesn't guarantee the attraction has lasting value. This Rocky of yours isn't a part of our social circle, so I won't lie and say I don't have my concerns. A common background is very important in building a relationship."

Carrie lowered her gaze.

Her mother reached out to grip Carrie's chin and raise her face. "Promise me you'll go slowly. Think things through before you make a commitment to this man."

Carrie met her mother's gaze squarely. "I'm doing more than thinking, Mom. I'm praying. If Rocky is the right person for me, then I trust God to help us work out all the differences we might encounter."

Lynette Steinwood drew back, her expression closed. "Just be careful."

Carrie nodded. "I will." But inwardly she rebelled — just once she wished she could simply trust and move forward without worry about hidden motives. Would God grant her that peace?

EIGHT

Carrie spritzed apple-scented body spray into the air then stepped into the mist, giving herself a subtle essence of the fragrance. One last glance in the full-length mirror, and she decided she was suitably attired for an evening at the Ironstone. It wasn't a fancy place, so her denim capris, saucy pink T-shirt with lime-green rhinestones imbedded around the V-neck, and rhinestone-studded pink flip-flops would be appropriate. She'd pulled her hair back into a ponytail and tied it with a pink and lime-green scarf. The thick ponytail swished back and forth across her shoulders as she bounced down the stairs.

Rounding the corner from the hallway to the kitchen, she heard her stepfather call her name. She turned back, resisting a glance at her wristwatch. She didn't want to be late.

"Yes, Mac? I'm on my way out." She offered a quick smile and remained poised to leave, one hand on the kitchen's swinging door, hoping he'd take the hint.

"I can see that." His gaze roved from her head to her toes then back again. "But not to anything formal, I assume."

Carrie felt a blush building, but she forced another smile. "No. Nothing formal. Just pizza with a friend."

Mac crossed his arms and peered down his nose at her. His pale green eyes narrowed into probing slits, making Carrie feel much younger than her twenty-four years. She fought the urge to squirm.

"This friend — would it happen to be the gentleman in whom your mother said you've expressed an interest?"

Carrie pressed her memory — what all had she said to Mom? Very little, truthfully. Mac was obviously digging for more information. She chose a casual tack. "Yes, as a matter of fact, it is, and I hate to keep him waiting, so if you don't mind —"

"Tell me about him."

Carrie drew in a breath, silently praying for patience. She knew her stepfather well enough to know he would keep her there until his curiosity had been satisfied. She might as well tell him what he wanted to know. Still, she'd give him the *Reader's*

Digest condensed version. "His name is Rocky Wilder, he's the groundskeeper for Elmwood Towers, and we've developed a friendship."

Mac stood for several long seconds, just looking into Carrie's eyes, his expression unreadable.

Carrie stood, looking back, waiting for Mac to make a disparaging remark or to suggest she change her plans. But his reply, when it came, surprised her.

"Well, if this is someone with whom you're taken, perhaps it's time for your mother and me to meet him."

Carrie's jaw dropped. Was he being serious? She looked at him carefully to determine whether he was teasing her. "You really want to meet him?"

Mac shrugged, a slow smile creeping up his cheek. It didn't light his eyes, but it did soften his austere appearance. "If you're going to be spending time with him, I think it's only proper that we become familiar with one another." He slid one hand into the pocket of his tailored navy dress slacks. "Would tomorrow night for dinner be too soon?"

"N–no. Tomorrow would be fine." Carrie's heart beat a hopeful double beat. If Mac approved the relationship, it would eliminate one major worry. "I'll ask him and see if he's free."

"Fine." Mac's smile widened; yet there seemed to be a cunning undertone in his expression. "Let's say dinner at seven, and that will give us time to visit a bit afterward. We can all become better acquainted."

Carrie nodded eagerly. "Yes. Thank you, Mac."

She smiled all the way to the Ironstone. The smile remained as she chose a corner booth, where she could watch the door for Rocky's arrival. She ordered a soft drink from the teen-age waitress then settled back to wait. A juke box played country tunes, and she hummed and sipped, waiting.

"Carrie!"

The enthusiastic greeting pulled Carrie's attention away from the door. She shifted her gaze to the left and found Angela's grinning face peering down at her from over the top of the partition which separated the booths. Carrie swallowed her groan of displeasure and pushed a smile into place.

"Well, hello, Angela. Are you here alone?" In a way Carrie hoped Angela wasn't alone — she didn't want to be obligated to ask Angela to join her. The girl's flushed face indicated she had been imbibing something.

"Me? Alone?" Angela pretended great

shock then laughed raucously. "No, I'm here with Janine, Ted, and Alex." Alex's head popped up next to Angela's. Angela gave him a kiss on the cheek, giggled when he tried to return the kiss, then pushed him away. Alex sank out of sight as Angela said, "But you seem to be alone. Come join us, girl!"

Carrie shook her head as a burst of laughter sounded from the other side of the partition. They must have already consumed a pitcher of beer; they were all so obnoxiously jolly. She had no desire to be a part of that, not even as a witness. So she shook her head. "No, thanks. You all enjoy yourselves. I'll just wait for my d—." She managed to stop herself from saying date and ended lamely, "Friend."

"The gardener you told me about?"

Carrie cringed at Angela's strident tone. She gave a quick nod in reply, praying Angela would drop the subject.

"Suit yourself." Angela shrugged and disappeared, leaving Carrie alone.

Carrie whispered a thank-you for the answer to her prayer, but the laughter and loud conversation continued, making Carrie feel more and more alone as time slipped by and Rocky still didn't appear.

Where could he be? Each time the sleigh

bells hanging above the door jingled the arrival of someone new, her heart leapt with eagerness. And each time someone other than Rocky entered the restaurant, her heart plummeted with disappointment and worry. She certainly hoped nothing had happened to him.

She finished her first soft drink, ordered a refill, ignored the raised eyebrows of the waitress when she repeated she wouldn't order food until her friend arrived, and waited some more.

Angela, hanging on Alex's arm, came around from the partition. She stopped beside Carrie's booth and tossed her head, swinging her auburn hair back over her shoulder. In a voice loud enough for the entire place to hear, she said, "Well, good-bye, Carrie. I sure hope your gardener shows up. Otherwise won't you look silly?" She released a shrill, brittle laugh.

Alex sent Carrie an apologetic look. "She's had one too many, kiddo. Ignore her." He gave Angela a tug that nearly sent her nose first to the floor. "Come on. You're making a fool of yourself."

"Me?" Angela's voice pierced an octave higher than usual. "I'm not the one who's sitting alone. I have a date!" She poked Alex in the chest with her long fingernail. "That's you, remember?" She squinted at Alex and said, "You aren't a gardener, are you?" She giggled again, peeking back at Carrie. Leaning in close, she lowered her voice to a raspy whisper. "This is what happens when you date gardeners, Carrie, dear. They aren't dependable. Remember that."

Alex jerked Angela away from Carrie. "Come on. I'm taking you home. 'Bye, Carrie." He led her out of the restaurant, with Janine and Ted following.

Carrie watched them go, her face burning as she realized how many people had turned to stare at Angela's display. She tried to pretend she didn't notice, just sipped her pop and drummed her fingernails on the checkered tablecloth, but eventually embarrassment got the best of her.

She waved the waitress over and said with a tight smile, "Something must have come up with my friend." She dropped a five-dollar bill on the table and rose. "Keep the change." Lifting her head high to retain what was left of her dignity, she strode out of the restaurant. Outside, she wilted against the brick exterior and allowed tears of mortification to fill her eyes. But she didn't let them fall. She blinked them away.

Surely Rocky didn't stand her up on purpose. Surely something happened. But why hadn't he called the restaurant and let her know? Sniffing, she pushed off from the building and headed to her car. She'd make a few phone calls, check to make sure he was okay. And if he was — well, she'd decide how to handle that after she'd figured out what kept him away.

Rocky marked another passage with a yellow highlighting pen, rubbed his eyes and looked up at the clock. Again. Eight-fifteen. By now Carrie had probably given up and gone home. Regret twisted his stomach. It had been cruel not showing up, but sometimes you had to be cruel to be kind. Wasn't that what the old song said anyway?

With a sigh he reread the passage he had been studying. One tiny phrase in Psalm 49 stood out — "rich and poor, together." He leaned back in his second-hand recliner, closed the Bible and released a sigh. Rich and poor together wasn't a concept he could grasp. Maybe in God's eyes, he conceded, the rich and the poor were equal and therefore could be together, but in man's eyes? Rocky couldn't imagine it happening.

Last Wednesday, seeing Carrie's friend behind the wheel of an SUV that probably cost more than a year's income as groundskeeper had been enough to convince him he had to back off. Caroline Mays Stein-wood belonged with somebody who could buy SUVs and wear designer clothes and keep his fingernails clean.

He lifted a piece of paper on which he'd scribbled Carrie's name then his own below it. The pairing looked odd on paper. It was beyond odd in person. He dropped the paper and pressed his palms to his Bible. At least he had acceptance with God. He belonged to God's family. God called him a son.

Despite his despondency over Carrie, joy pressed upward as he considered being an adopted son in God's own family. And Carrie was a daughter. That made them brother and sister in Christ. He toyed with the idea. Could they be friends as brothers and sisters in Christ? Could they have a relationship that was strictly friendship? He'd told Carrie how special it was to be friends with her, and he'd meant it. He'd never eased into a relationship the way he had with Carrie. Their time together had been unique, special, and after only a few days of separation he missed it. He missed *her.* . . .

He set the Bible on the end table and rose, crossing to the window to peer out at the darkening landscape. The closest neighbor was more than a mile down the road, and the lights in their windows looked like wavering dots from this distance. That was okay, though. He didn't mind being alone. At least he hadn't minded until lately. Until Carrie.

Pushing off from the window frame, he stomped to the television and snapped it on. But after scrolling through the few channels that came through, he found nothing of worth to watch. He jammed his thumb on the OFF button, dropped the remote and sat back in his chair.

The moment his backside connected with the chair seat, the phone rang.

And Rocky knew without a doubt it was Carrie.

He sat, frozen, holding his breath, as the telephone blared. *Ri-i-ing . . . ri-i-ing . . . ri-i-ing. . . .* But he didn't answer it. After ten rings it stopped, and he blew out the air he'd been holding. He sat in tense silence, his shoulder muscles aching, while he waited to see if it would start again.

Nothing.

His throat felt dry, so he pushed himself out of the chair and headed to the kitchen. While he held a glass under the water spigot, the phone began blaring again. *Ri-i-ing . . . ri-i-ing . . . ri-i-ing. . . .*

Water splashed over the rim of the glass

and across his hand. He smacked the handle down and raised the glass to his lips, gulping water as if he hadn't had his thirst quenched in years. At the last swallow the phone stopped.

"Whew." He put the glass in the sink and hung his head low, his hands braced on the edge of the counter. Before it could start again, he'd have to get out of here. Go see Eileen? No, it was Friday — she and several residents got together for a red hat tea every Friday evening. Philip and his wife, Marin, might be home, but they were still pretty much newlyweds. He hated to intrude uninvited. He'd given up most of his other friendships when he'd accepted Christ. Where could he go?

Loneliness struck hard, and he wished he'd just gone to the pizza place to see Carrie one more time before deciding he couldn't do it anymore. He stomped again to the window and peered across the acreage he'd purchased. In his mind's eye he envisioned rows of hybrid irises and roses and shrubs — his own plantings which could be transplanted into other people's yards. He had the space. He just needed the know-how.

Suddenly he knew how to fill the remainder of his evening. The public library was open until ten on weekday nights. He'd go in, do some research on the internet, find out if any correspondence courses were available in landscaping, check out some books on starting a business. He'd engross himself in his future plans. That should help him forget his past, brief relationship with Carrie Mays.

Just as he snatched his keys off the end of the kitchen counter, the phone started to ring again. His hand hovered over the receiver, the temptation to answer nearly overwhelming. *Please, God, give me the strength to let her go. She's too good for a no-good wild boy like me.* He balled his hand into a fist, ordered himself to ignore the sound, and headed out the door.

Carrie slammed her telephone onto her mattress. Why didn't he answer? When, out of concern, she had called his brother, Philip had assured her nothing was wrong. As Rocky's next of kin he'd have been notified if there had been an accident. As far as Philip knew, Rocky was spending his evening at home.

But Rocky was supposed to have spent his evening with her!

Fury filled her as she remembered sitting in that booth, straining toward the door at every jingle of those bells. Angela had said she looked ridiculous, and Angela was right. She had been ridiculous to wait that long for Rocky to show up.

She yanked the scarf from her ponytail, and her hair fell in an unruly tumble across her shoulders. Impatiently she shoved the strands behind her ears. She yanked drawers open, pulling out clean pajama pants and a T-shirt for bed. Changing with jerky motions, she deposited her clothes into the hamper the way a basketball star deposits a slam dunk. Then she flumped across the bed, crossed her ankles, folded her arms, and glared across the room for several minutes, letting the anger keep the hurt at bay.

But it couldn't last. In time the fury faded, and all that was left was a feeling of intense betrayal. Another man had let her down. And she suspected that, once again, it had to do with her money. But this time, instead of the man trying to find a way to get to it, she was pretty sure Rocky was trying to get away from it.

When she'd told him her full name, his reaction spoke of intense discomfort. It didn't take a rocket scientist to figure out Rocky felt inferior to her. Although she'd feared that he, like so many others, might chase her for her money, it now appeared her money was chasing him off.

"Why, God? Why can't I find a man who looks at me and only sees me, not the money I have? I just want to be loved for *me*. . . ."

She rolled onto her side and cuddled a plump pillow, hugging it against her chest as she tried to overcome the pressing desire to cry. But despite her best effort she didn't succeed.

NINE

Carrie lifted a bite of Myrna's succulent beef roast to her mouth, chewed and swallowed. But she might as well have been eating shredded paper for the enjoyment she found in the meal. Her parents sat at opposite ends of the dining table, candlelight flickering across their faces, as they exchanged occasional glances. Conversation lagged, and Carrie knew why. The empty seat across the table from her — the seat in which Rocky would be sitting had she been able to invite him — provided a tremendous distraction.

Although neither Mac nor her mother had quizzed her when she said he wouldn't be joining them, Carrie knew the question was rife in both their minds. She had no desire to address the issue because she'd have to admit she'd been stood up. The humiliation still stung. She'd tried calling Rocky off and on all day, still with no answer, and the acute sadness that had brought on her tears last night had changed once more to anger. At least the anger was easier to carry than the sadness had been.

Myrna came in quietly to clear away the plates then served dessert — apple pie with scoops of vanilla ice cream sprinkled with cinnamon. The cook looked into Carrie's eyes when she placed the warmed dessert dish on the table, and Carrie rewarded her with a smile. She appreciated Myrna's attempt to cheer her up. Even if this pie was flavorless, she would consume every bite, for Myrna's sake.

When Myrna returned to the kitchen, Mac leaned his elbows on the table and fixed Carrie with a dour look. "Well, I'd say it's time to talk."

Lynette raised her gaze and suggested, "Should it wait until after dessert?"

But Mac shook his head. "I've waited long enough. She needs to know."

Carrie's heart leapt into her throat. Fear assaulted her so fiercely she dropped her fork. "What?" She looked frantically back and forth at her parents. "What do I need to know? Is it about Rocky?" Oh, something was wrong! Something had happened to Rocky! She clasped her trembling hands together and pressed them into her lap, the dessert forgotten. "Tell me, Mac, please."

Mac pursed his lips for a moment, his eyes turning steely. He took in a deep breath. "I've done some checking on this grounds-keeper from Elmwood Towers. When you mentioned his name last night, I was certain I'd heard it somewhere before. I was right."

Carrie processed Mac's remarks. From what he had just said, she gathered nothing had happened to Rocky. A feeling of relief washed over her, followed by a wave of anger. If nothing was wrong, he should be here! She nearly missed Mac's next comment.

"Are you aware that when Rocky Wilder was a young man he stole several hundred dollars' worth of lumber from one of the Steinwood building sites?"

Carrie blinked, staring at her stepfather. That explained why his name had seemed familiar when he'd told her. Now she remembered how Mac had raved about some juvenile delinquent who dared to walk off with his property. Still, she couldn't see Rocky doing that. "Stole? From you?"

Mac nodded grimly. "That's correct. He was caught red-handed, taken into custody and spent six weeks in a juvenile detention center." Mac leaned back, propping one elbow on the high back of his chair. "It would have been more had the lumber not been recovered, completely undamaged."

"Carrie, darling, I know you're taken with this man" — Carrie's mother spoke softly — "but perhaps you should give this relationship some serious thought. My main concern when we spoke was the differences in your backgrounds, but now, with what Mac has uncovered . . ." Lynette pursed her mouth in sympathy. "It doesn't seem wise, to me, to pursue someone who so clearly lacks scruples."

Carrie spun back to Mac. "How old was Rocky when this happened?"

Mac waved his hand as if it didn't matter, but Carrie leaned forward, intent on having her question answered. Finally Mac huffed. "Junior high age, I believe — thirteen or fourteen." Then he pointed at her. "But that's beside the point. The point is the man is a thief. To be honest, I'm not sure I want him to continue as an employee at Elmwood Towers. What's to keep him from pilfering things from the residents there?"

Carrie's hackles rose. Her stepfather was being unfairly judgmental, and she couldn't let his comments pass. "Rocky does an excellent job as groundskeeper. The landscaping is beautifully done, and the residents adore him. He's friends with them.

Please don't interfere in his job there."

Mac shook his head. "Carrie, you are hopelessly naïve. I might admire your desire to look for the good in people, but good simply does not exist in some people. That Wilder boy is one of those people. He's rotten to the core." His imperious finger aimed in her direction again. "He's after your money, Carrie, plain and simple. He smelled it the minute he spotted you, and he plotted from the beginning how to win you so he could get at your wealth."

Carrie rose from the table, heat filling her face. She prayed for control as she forced a quiet tone. "You're wrong, Mac. If Rocky were after my money, he'd be sitting in that chair right now, doing his best to impress you and win you over. But he isn't there, is he? He didn't show. He didn't show because he's scared to death of my money. He knows he doesn't have any, and he thinks that makes him unworthy. *You* think that makes him unworthy. But I don't. In God's eyes we're all equal, and —"

Mac waved his hand, rolling his eyes. "Don't bring God into it, Carrie."

"I have to bring God into it," she insisted, surprising herself with her boldness. "I can't set Him aside. He's a part of me." She took a step toward her stepfather and touched his arm. "Mac, I know you're only acting out of concern for me, and I want you to know I appreciate it. But you've got to understand — you're wrong about Rocky."

Mac jerked his arm away and thrust out his jaw. "I don't believe I am."

"Think about it." Carrie used her best persuasive tone, swinging her gaze back and forth to include both of her parents. "If he wanted something from me, wouldn't he be pursuing me? Instead he's running away. Doesn't that prove anything to you?"

Mac stood and tossed his napkin on the table. He towered over Carrie with flashing eyes. "It proves to me he's wily enough to have found a way to hoodwink you. And you're foolish enough to fall for it." He raised both hands in defeat. "Fine, Carrie. Believe what you want to believe. But when he's absconded with your trust fund and left you crying in a gutter, don't come creeping to me for a handout. The agreement your mother and I reached was that when your inheritance from your father became available, you are no longer my concern. My responsibility toward you ends on your twenty-fifth birthday, young woman, so don't anticipate receiving a penny of Steinwood assets. And you'd better carefully consider how much you trust that Wilder boy."

Without giving Carrie a chance to reply, he turned and stomped from the room. His final words had struck like blows, leaving Carrie feeling as though her heart was bruised. She turned to her mother, and her voice quivered as she asked, "Is what he just said true? You discussed my no longer being a part of the Steinwood family after I turn twenty-five?"

"Now, Carrie, there is enough money in the trust fund set up with your father's assets to —"

"It isn't the money I'm worried about, Mother!" Carrie could hardly believe what she was hearing. Couldn't anyone see beyond the money to the relationship? "I've spent the last twenty years in this house. I know Mac and I have had our differences, but he's the only father I know. He plans to simply cut me loose when I no longer need his financial support?"

Her mother lowered her gaze, refusing to answer. That gave Carrie all the answer she needed. Rejected. Again. Her heart ached with the implication. She muttered, "I've got to get out of here." She headed for the door. She heard her mother call her name — she heard the apology in her tone — but she ignored it and kept going. Obviously she could not depend on her mother and stepfather. She had to find out whether she could depend on Rocky.

Rocky gave an all-body stretch that lifted his feet from the footrest of the recliner. He set the gardening book he'd been reading aside and padded to the kitchen. Removing a bottle of pop from his fridge, he unscrewed the top and drank directly from the bottle. Just as he placed the bottle back on the shelf, someone knocked on his front door.

Frowning, he glanced at the clock. Who would be out here now? A couple of years ago his friends dropped by at all hours, cases of beer in hand, ready to party. But visitors were few and far between now that he'd given up those wild habits. He crossed to the door and swung it wide then nearly fell backward when he saw who stood on the metal steps that served as his porch.

"Carrie?"

She didn't wait for an invitation, just opened the screen door and stepped in as if she'd been there a dozen times before. Embarrassment washed over him as he took in her neat appearance. Her pale orange pants, just high enough to show off her shapely ankles, and the sleeveless top sporting pastel-colored squares on a white background made him think of a garden styled by Van Gogh. Standing there in his cut-off jeans shorts and missing-sleeves T-shirt, he wished he could dive behind the recliner and hide.

"Hi, Rocky. I'm sorry to intrude on you this way, but I couldn't reach you by telephone."

Her sweet voice held none of the loathing he deserved for his despicable treatment. The desire to hide increased. "Yeah. . . ." He scratched his head. "I've been —" But he had no excuse, and he wouldn't lie to her. He blew out a lengthy breath and admitted, "I haven't been answering my phone." He frowned. "How did you know where to find me?"

She raised one eyebrow. "Your brother, Philip, gave me directions. He's a nice guy."

He wondered if that last comment was meant to be a barb. If so, he deserved it. He let it pass. "Well, come on in and sit down. It's nothing fancy." What an understatement. How could his used trailer, although he kept it clean, hope to compare to the mansion in which she lived? Still, she showed no disdain as she crossed to the afghan-draped sofa and seated herself.

Rocky perched in his recliner, but he left it upright. He found himself blurting out,

"I'm sorry I don't have a nicer house. I thought maybe one day I'd build one out here, but in the meantime . . ."

Carrie shook her head, a soft smile on her face. "Rocky, quit apologizing. I don't care what kind of house you live in. All I care about is you. And I have to tell you, you had me worried when you didn't show up last night as we'd planned. I was afraid something had happened to you."

Rocky hung his head, guilt striking hard. He should have considered that. He hadn't meant to worry her. "I'm sorry about that." He hoped she knew he meant it.

"What happened?"

He brought his head up to meet her gaze. She looked so sweet and concerned, no hint of the anger she should be feeling evident in her eyes. He couldn't answer her, though. He needed to know something. "Carrie, why do you care at all about me?"

The question seemed to startle her. She straightened, her eyes widening, her lips parting as if searching for words. After a moment she asked, her voice filled with confusion, "Is there some reason why I shouldn't?"

Rocky stood and threw his arms outward. "There're at least a dozen reasons why you shouldn't! Look at me. Look at this place.

Then look at yourself. What do you want with me?"

"Your friendship." The answer came quickly.

"Why?" He fired the word.

She offered a soft laugh, lifting her shoulders in a graceful shrug. "I don't know. I just know I do. I like you, Rocky."

Her words took the bones out of his legs. At least that's how he felt. Suddenly they couldn't hold him up anymore. He sat back in his chair and shook his head, amazed. He admitted, "I like you, too, Carrie."

"Then why'd you let me down?"

For the first time he heard genuine pain in her voice. Without conscious thought he reached for her. Her hand met his and clung hard. In her grasp he sensed the hurt he'd caused her, and his chest tightened in remorse.

"I'm so sorry, Carrie. I shouldn't have left you sitting there alone last night. It was cowardly of me. But when I saw you with that man Wednesday night —"

"Man? You mean Carl?"

Rocky shrugged. "I don't know his name. He showed up at the end of the Bible study and followed you home. When I saw you with him, I just thought you two . . . I don't know . . . *fit*. And I knew I didn't. Not with you. Not like he does. So . . . I backed off."

She gave his hand a tug. "Rocky, whatever you thought you saw, Carl and I most certainly do *not* fit. He has no use for God, and that's reason enough for me to keep my distance. But there's more. Carl wants me to believe he's interested in me, but I happen to know he's most interested in my money." She lowered her gaze, her forehead creasing. But when she lifted her head again, her expression had cleared. "I can't be with someone who only wants what I can give, monetarily. Does that make sense?"

Rocky thought about what she'd said. He had to admit, the idea of all that wealth was appealing. He wouldn't be honest if he said otherwise. Yet there was so much more to Carrie than her wealth. The fact that she'd come looking for him, was worried about him, told him a great deal about her heart. He nodded. "Yes. It makes sense."

"Good." She withdrew her hand and tipped her head, fixing him with a steady gaze. "I forgive you for standing me up last night, but you do owe me."

He felt a grin tug at his cheek. "Oh yeah?"

"Yes. I got no supper last night because of you."

"I'm really sorry about that, Carrie."

"Prove it."

He raised one brow. "How?"

"Buy me lunch. Tomorrow. I want sandwiches and fruit at the park. You know where the duck pond is?"

He nodded.

"One o'clock at the duck pond. Tuna salad with raw spinach. Golden Delicious apples with caramel dip. And lemonade to drink."

He couldn't help himself. A chuckle rumbled from his chest. She didn't pull any punches, and he liked it. "And that'll serve as a proper apology?"

"As long as the apples are crisp, not mealy," she retorted with a grin.

He laughed out loud. "Okay, Carrie, you've got it. I'll be there."

She looked at him, her expression suddenly wary. "Really? You'll be there?"

He saw the insecurity lurking beneath the surface. It pained him how much his failure to show up last night had cost her. He took her hand and said earnestly, "I'll be there."

She smiled and rose. "Good. See you tomorrow, Rocky." She slipped out the door.

He sure hoped the grocery store had some fresh, crisp, Golden Delicious apples in their produce department.

TEN

Rocky didn't bother to change out of his church clothes before meeting Carrie. She'd said be there by one o'clock, and he was determined to be early so there'd be no question in her mind as to whether he was coming. The grocery store not only had crisp Golden Delicious apples, but it also had a deli with tuna salad, so he had the sandwiches made there. On impulse he grabbed a loaf of white bread from the day-old case. Carrie could feed it to the ducks.

He found half-liter bottles of lemonade in the cooler beside the check-out counter, paid for his purchases and piled everything in a plastic grocery sack. Nothing fancy, but he knew Carrie wouldn't mind. It was one of the things he admired about her — she didn't put on airs.

When he arrived at the park, several other people were already gathered in small clusters or pairs, but he didn't see Carrie.

He walked to the duck pond and sat gingerly on the grass. He didn't want grass stains on his good pants. He heard a burst of laughter from one of the groups, and it made him feel lonely as he sat by himself. Suddenly insecurity hit. Would Carrie come? Not showing up would be a good pay-back for what he'd done to her last Friday night. But as quickly as the fear stabbed, he pushed it aside. Carrie wasn't vindictive. She'd be here.

He was right. He'd no more than had the thought when he heard her sweet voice from behind him.

"You're right on time."

Peeking over his shoulder, he watched her approach, graceful in a pair of strappy sandals and flowing sundress. Her hair lay loose across her shoulders, the sun catching the shimmering strands of blond. It struck him again how beautiful she was. And she wanted to be with him. He didn't deserve her at all.

He rose and greeted her with a quick, impersonal hug, wishing he had the courage to give her a kiss. "You look so pretty — too fancy for a picnic."

She smiled and flipped his tie with the ends of her fingers. "What about you? You look like an executive in your tie."

He felt a blush building, but it was strictly due to pleasure, not embarrassment. Who else would tell Rocky Wilder he looked like an executive? Uncertain how to reply, he changed the subject. "I'm sorry I didn't bring a blanket or anything. I'm afraid you'll get your dress dirty."

"Did you bring the food?"

"Oh yeah. Just what you asked for."

"Then I'm satisfied," she said, and her smile proved it.

"Well, then, here." He removed the items from the bag then pressed the square of plastic flat against the grass. "You sit on this. At least it'll protect your skirt."

"Thanks." She flashed him another smile and seated herself. Her movements were so graceful, Rocky felt like a clod plunking down beside her.

He handed her a sandwich and bottle of lemonade, leaving the bag of apples and tub of caramel dip in his lap. "These can be dessert," he said, indicating the apples.

"Perfect." She tipped her head. "Do you want to say grace?"

He nodded and bowed his head. "Dear Lord, thank You for the beautiful day, the beautiful companion, and this picnic lunch. Bless the food so it may nourish us to do Your service. Amen." Although praying in

135

front of others usually made him self-conscious, it seemed natural with Carrie. When he opened his eyes, he found Carrie's gaze fixed on him.

"That was perfect, Rocky. Thank you."

"You're welcome." He swallowed, forcing his focus away from her beguiling blue eyes and to his sandwich. "Better eat. The breeze'll dry out your bread."

Two ducks waddled in their direction, and Rocky handed Carrie the loaf of day-old bread. "I think your friends are hungry. They'll take your sandwich if you aren't careful. Throw them some of that bread."

She laughed. "What a wonderful idea!" She opened the loaf, tore one piece in half and tossed it to the ducks. Their happy clamor immediately drew a crowd. Carrie had the bag empty in no time, but the ducks quacked for more. She looked at Rocky with raised brows. "Now what?"

"Greedy quackers," he muttered. "Well, I'm not giving them my lunch. Come on. Maybe if we move off a bit, they'll get the hint and go bother someone else."

Fortunately his suggestion proved true. When they moved to a picnic table in the shade, the ducks waddled off toward another group of picnickers. Carrie watched them go, a soft smile curving her lips.

"I haven't fed the ducks in years. Not since I was a very little girl. My dad brought me to the park to feed the ducks." She turned to look at Rocky, and he saw a hint of sadness in the depth of her eyes. "He's been gone for twenty years, but sometimes I still think about him."

"Yeah. Mine died four years ago. I think of him sometimes too." He didn't add that the memories weren't pleasant ones.

"Mom married Mac less than a year after Dad's death. He and my dad had been friends. Mac isn't nearly as warm and loving as my dad was, but at least I've had someone in that role." Carrie took a bite of her sandwich and chewed, her expression thoughtful. "Dads are pretty important people, you know? I've been thinking about the Bible study at church. I didn't realize how much a dad can influence how you see God."

Rocky frowned, not sure he understood what she meant. "How so?"

She pursed her lips for a moment. "Well, for instance, if you grew up with a very loving, protective dad, you'd see God as loving and protective. But if you grew up with a distant dad, one who only talked to you when you did something wrong, then you'd see God as a punitive figure, only there to make you feel shamed."

Rocky considered this. His dad had been hard, unyielding in his expectations, rarely affectionate. When he'd first heard about God, he couldn't imagine that God would care about him. Now he wondered how much of that idea came from his relationship with his father. He remembered how he'd resisted even thinking of God as Father. Carrie must be right.

She went on. "Mac hasn't been all that loving, but I do have my memories of my real dad, and all of those are good. That must be where I based my ideas of God, because as soon as someone told me about God I was ready to embrace Him." She flashed him a smile. "Being a Christian, being part of God's family, is the best thing I can think of."

"Even better than being rich," Rocky remarked, recalling how all his life he'd simply wanted wealth. Now it didn't seem to matter so much. But his words made Carrie flinch. He touched her arm. "What's wrong?"

She put her sandwich down, her head low. "It's always about money. . . ."

Rocky regretted his impulsive words, but he hadn't meant them the way she took them. He tugged her arm, encouraging her to look up. "Carrie, I'm sorry I said that. It had more to do with me, and the way I used to be, than you."

She looked at him with pain in her eyes. "You mean you can honestly look at me and not see my money?"

He pulled his hand back, searching for a truthful reply. His voice faltered as he answered. "Carrie, I like you. I really do. You're sweet and pretty and fun. And when I just think of you as Carrie, I'm okay. It's when the other intrudes — the realization that Carrie is also Caroline Steinwood — that's when I have trouble."

Carrie nodded miserably. She suspected as much. It was unfair that Mac looked at Rocky and only saw the bad things Rocky had done. It was just as unfair that people looked at her and only saw her money. How to overcome those preconceived notions? She didn't know. The happy feeling of picnicking with Rocky drifted away, replaced by regret. Maybe they'd never be able to overcome the issue of her money.

Well, if they were to try, Rocky would need to know the whole truth. She raised her gaze to look directly into his eyes. Their warm, velvety depths, open and attentive, gave her the courage she needed.

"Rocky, in less than a month, I'll turn twenty-five." He opened his mouth to say something, but she held up her hand. "And you need to know what happens then. My father was a very wealthy man. When he died, he left nearly everything in a trust fund for me. Sometimes I think that's why my mom married Mac — Daddy provided for my future, but it was my distant future, and he left very little to Mom for the present. She needed Mac's money to survive. So did I.

"But on my twenty-fifth birthday the trust fund becomes truly mine to do with as I please. I won't be dependent on Mac anymore, and I won't need to be. I'll be very wealthy in my own right." She searched Rocky's face. He didn't so much as blink. She continued. "I need to know if this causes a problem for you."

He drew in a long breath, his gaze drifting to the side for a moment as he appeared to gather his thoughts. When he turned back to face her, she was frightened by what she saw in his eyes. She was certain it was remorse.

"Carrie, I have to be honest. When I was growing up, I had very little. I guess that's why I stole — I wanted what other people had. I thought those things would make me happy. Of course they didn't. I didn't recognize it at the time, but I think my own guilt made me unable to enjoy the things I took. The best thing that happened to me was getting caught stealing and being forced to face the consequences of my actions. I never stole again, but I still wanted things."

He shook his head, a lopsided smile appearing. "Do you know I used to stand outside the fence of your house, wishing I lived in the Steinwood mansion?"

"You did?" She wondered why she'd never seen him.

A quick nod made his hair slip across his forehead. He ran his fingers through the strands, smoothing them back in place. "Yes. I wanted your house. I wanted your money. I wanted . . . everything you had. I thought I'd surely be happy if all those things were mine. For years that's all I thought about — becoming wealthy. Becoming happy."

He shrugged. "Obviously I haven't become wealthy. I work as a gardener and live in a trailer house. About as unwealthy as a person can be." He chuckled a bit at his own expense. "And for the most part I think I managed to get past that dream of being rich. Until I met you." He shook his head, whistling through his teeth. "Boy, I don't know how to explain this."

Although Carrie's heart beat in trepidation, she said, "Try. I'm listening."

"I think I managed to find contentment in just being Rocky Wilder, groundskeeper, but then you came along in your fancy clothes and your fancy car, and suddenly being groundskeeper wasn't enough again. I wanted more. But not for *me* this time, for you. I like you, and I want to give you things. Things like you're used to having. And I can't do that. So . . ."

"So that's why you avoided me Friday night? Because you can't give me things?" She wanted to make sure she understood.

He nodded. The strand of hair slipped again, and it was all Carrie could do to keep from guiding it into place for him. "Yeah. I can't compete with all you have, Carrie. And it hurts my pride, you know? Even if I get my business up and running, it'll only be a landscaping business. Nothing like what you want to do with your life — executive position, using computers and all that." He huffed in aggravation, his forehead creased. "I'm nobody compared to you."

His last statement made her mad. "You aren't *nobody,* Rocky. Not compared to me or anyone else. Do you think God sees you as a nobody? No. He sees you as His creation, and He loves you just the way you are. You've got to stop putting yourself down because you don't have money. It isn't right."

"It also isn't easy," he shot back.

She nodded, acknowledging his words. "I know. But you have to *try,* Rocky. Because if you don't, we . . ." She turned her gaze away. Was there a "we" where she and Rocky were concerned?

After several quiet minutes she turned back. "I don't want my money to come between us. Is it going to?"

He rested his chin in his hand, his gaze pinned on hers, while he seemed to struggle with forming an answer. Finally an answer came, but it wasn't the one Carrie hoped for. "I don't know. I want to see just you — Carrie, my friend — but Caroline Mays Steinwood keeps getting in the way."

"So think about something else!" She threw her hands outward, disgusted with his short-sightedness. "Think about . . . your own landscaping business and what it will take to get it running. Don't even think about me and my goals. Focus on your own."

"But don't you see I can't? They're all intermingling!" He appeared as frustrated as she felt. He rammed his hand through his hair. "When I think of me landscaping, the picture ends up side by side with you in a business suit in a meeting with multimillionaires. I think of my trailer house, and your family's mansion looms over it. I think of my past, all the wrong things I did, and when I compare that to your sweetness . . . The two don't fit together, Carrie — don't you see?"

"All I see," she said, blinking to hold back tears, "is that you're going to ruin something good if you don't let go of my money. The money doesn't mean that much to me, Rocky. But if it means that much to you it's always going to be in the way. And we don't stand a chance of making this relationship work."

"I know." The simple answer came out in a groan.

Although Carrie recognized how deeply Rocky wanted to make things work, she also knew it was not going to happen easily. She took his hand. The calluses on his palm and the ends of each finger felt scratchy against her flesh. She squeezed hard to let him know they didn't bother her.

"Rocky, please. I need someone who will see me for who I am. Not Caroline Mays, recipient of a massive trust fund. Not Caroline Steinwood, stepdaughter of Mac Steinwood. Not rich-girl Carrie. Just . . . *Carrie.* Can you do that?"

He met her gaze, his fingers tightening on hers. "I can try." His voice sounded raspy. He cleared his throat and added, "I'll do my best."

Carrie wasn't sure that was good enough, but for now it would have to do. She turned to watch a pair of ducks glide across the pond toward one another. They touched beaks then continued side by side. She sighed. All the people in the world who thought money was the answer to their problems. If they only knew the problem money could be. . . . Her mouth felt dry, and she licked her lips.

Rocky bumped her arm with a bottle of lemonade. "It won't stay cold much longer. Better drink it."

She took it, but it was slippery from condensation, and she nearly dropped it. Rocky recovered it by grasping both the bottle and her hand. Their gazes collided for a moment, and she allowed him a glimpse of her agony. She saw a matching sadness in his eyes, too.

"Do you have it?" he asked, his voice barely above a whisper.

"Yes." She pulled her hand away, the bottle secure. She unscrewed the cap and lifted the bottle to her lips for a sip of the sweet, cool liquid. It soothed her throat, but her heart remained burdened.

She had prayed for God to bring a man into her life who wouldn't pursue her for her money. She never dreamed she'd need to pray for one to accept it.

ELEVEN

Carrie slipped in the back door and headed directly to her bedroom. No servants were around — Sunday was their day off. Her mother's suite door was closed, indicating she was taking her Sunday afternoon nap, and Mac was nowhere in sight. That suited Carrie. She wanted some time alone.

She changed out of her dress and put it in with the wash going to the dry cleaners. For a moment she stood in her walk-in closet and let her gaze rove across the variety of clothing items available to her. So many fancy, unnecessary things. Her mother loved to dress her up — she always had. Mother glowed with pride when someone said, "What a pretty girl your Carrie is."

Carrie frowned. Would Mother have loved her as much had she been a plain-looking girl? She pushed that thought away and moved to her dresser, where she pulled out a pair of pajama pants and a T-shirt. Nothing fancy, but merely comfortable. In the privacy of her bedroom she could get by with that.

Climbing into the four-poster bed she stacked up the plump pillows and leaned into the comforting softness. How different Rocky had looked today. He had a rugged appeal in his work clothes that showed his developed biceps, wide shoulders, and narrow hips. But today, in a pair of pleated trousers, button-down oxford shirt, and tie of muted blues and greens, she'd been given a different glimpse of Rocky. Her heart thumped as she remembered the jolt of reaction that had attacked her middle when he'd turned and flashed his welcoming smile. Rocky in dress-up clothes was an arresting sight.

She sighed, shifting into a more reclined position, as she allowed her thoughts to drift, dissecting all the reasons she found Rocky desirable. His height and strong arms gave her a feeling of protection. She knew she was safe with him. Those moments when he'd hugged her — just one brief, almost impersonal embrace — had turned her insides to mush. If a hug did all that, what might a kiss do? She felt an embarrassed flush fill her face as she considered it. Would she ever find out?

Grabbing one of the pillows, she hugged it to her chest, an attempt to calm her accelerated heartbeat. She suspected he wouldn't be the aggressor. Angela had said he was a player in high school, but she saw none of that in his behavior. He was always a gentleman — flirtatious but respectful.

What would he do if she kissed him? She considered it, wondering if she could find the courage to be bold enough to kiss him. Always the men had pursued her, never the other way around. They'd pursued her because she was pretty, but also because she was rich.

Rocky wouldn't pursue her because she was rich. Her wealth left him feeling inadequate. She remembered the look in his eyes as he'd admitted he had a hard time separating Carrie his friend from Caroline Steinwood. She huffed in aggravation, throwing the pillow aside. Why couldn't he see her for herself? Just once, why couldn't someone see her for herself?

"It's always been this way." The words came out in a harsh whisper. She believed her mother loved her because she was attractive and intelligent — the perfect trophy child to put on exhibit for her friends. Mac provided for her to please her mother, not because of any real affection for her. The friends she'd had while growing up had spent time with her because it was prestigious to be invited to the Steinwood mansion. Carl had ardently pursued her because of the magnitude of her trust fund. Carrie's heart ached as she realized how many people cared for her to suit their own needs, not to meet her needs for love and affection.

Raising her gaze to the coffered ceiling, she spoke aloud. "Thank You, God, for loving me for me. Thank You for not loving me for what I could give You, but loving me just because. There isn't anyone else in my life who's done that. . . ."

Not even Rocky. Not honestly. It hurt her to acknowledge it. She believed Rocky was trying, but even with him the money created a diversion. Closing her eyes and lowering her head, she continued talking to her heavenly Father. But this prayer was one of desire. "Please, God, I'm falling in love with Rocky, and I believe he's falling in love with me. Let him look past the dollar signs to my heart. Let him see me — just me. . . ."

"Hand me another one of those mums." Eileen reached her gloved hand toward Rocky.

Rocky had promised to help her get a variety of mums planted before she needed to pick up the boys from work Monday afternoon. They'd spent nearly an hour together, with him pausing in the distribution of fertilizer to offer a hand when needed, and half the mums were already in the ground. He looked where she had the trowel poised now. "You gonna put it there?"

Eileen blinked at him, her lips pursed. "That was my intention. Why?"

He rose, his knees popping, and crossed to her in three long strides. He pointed. "If you put it that close to the rhododendron, it'll get the afternoon shade. Besides that, from this angle, it'll be nearly hidden. Since this garden will be mostly enjoyed from the bench on the other side of the walking path, I'd say shift it forward and to the left about twelve inches."

Eileen pushed to her feet and waddled to where he stood on the grass. Hands on hips, she looked at the garden area from his viewpoint. Then with a rueful chuckle she shook her head. "Okay, I concede. You're right." Squinting up at him, she gave him a playful poke on the shoulder. "You do know what you're doing, don't you?"

She bent over, snatched up one of the potted mums and returned to the garden spot to begin digging a hole to receive the plant.

While she dug, she asked, "So have you done any more checking on the classes you need to become a landscaper?"

Rocky pushed the fertilizer spreader back and forth, its gentle hum competing with the scratch of Eileen's trowel in the dirt. Good sounds. "I've checked. But . . ."

She sat back on her haunches, fixing him with a stern look. "But?"

He stopped, blew out a breath and shook his head. "But I don't know if it's worth it."

Eileen scowled, the lines around her mouth becoming pronounced. "What is *that* supposed to mean?"

"Aw, don't look at me like that," he protested, getting the spreader going again. "Think about it. There're all kinds of reasons to forget about that stupid dream. For one, I'm gonna be thirty years old in another year. I'm too old to be going to college — I'd look silly with all those young kids. Besides that, I'm too stupid. Barely made it through high school. How would I survive college classes on botany and biology and business? I'm just kidding myself."

"Rocky Wilder, you stop pushing that machine and come here."

The stern tone brought him to a halt. He looked at her and swallowed a grin. She was doing her best to appear fierce, but her fiercest was pretty tame compared to what Rocky grew up with. Still, he followed her direction just because he liked her so much.

She had to tip her head back to look him in the face. "It isn't the college that's got you running scared. You could handle the classes. You know you aren't stupid." Waving her arm to indicate the grounds, she said, "All the signs of your handiwork indicate you aren't stupid. You have the ability. So what's the problem?"

"It's just a silly dream!" The words burst out more forcefully than he intended.

"Why is it silly?" She matched his tone.

"Because it is."

"Well, that's a silly answer." She glared up at him, daring him to contradict her. "Do you think God gives silly talents? No, He plants in each of His children the ability to do *something,* and that 'something' is for good. Nothing silly about that. You bring beauty to our corner of the world, and I won't let you call it silly."

"But anybody could —"

"No, they couldn't! Look at what I nearly did with that mum. Would've hidden it in the shade. But not you — you could see the big picture. You're a natural, Rocky, and you need to use that talent."

Rocky dropped his chin, shaking his head.

"Look, Eileen — it was fun to think about, but it just isn't realistic."

She waved her hand in dismissal. "You're too hard on yourself. You could handle those classes if you wanted to. It isn't unrealistic to expect yourself to succeed in school."

"It's not just that," he blurted out, surprising himself.

"Then what is it? Spill it."

He swallowed. "I–I want a family, Eileen. I want a family I can take care of. *Really* take care of. Not just give 'em the basics, but give 'em the extras, you know what I mean? Vacations and braces" — he ran his tongue over his crooked teeth — "and a nice house. Even if I get a business started, even if I do landscaping for other people as my job, I'm still nothing more than a glorified gardener. I'll never be rich, not rich enough to do all those things for my family."

Eileen listened intently, her brow creased. "That's really important to you?"

"Yes!" He flung his arms outward. "I spent all my growing-up years feeling envious of the kids who had nice clothes and new bicycles every year for Christmas and silver braces making their teeth straight. I don't want my own kids feeling that way."

"Oh, Rocky. . . ." Eileen shook her head, a

sad smile softening the lines around her mouth. "Sit down here with me for a minute, huh?"

They sat side by side in the grass, while the early fall sun heated their heads. Eileen plucked one strand of grass and used it to point at him.

"I understand why you feel the way you do, but I think you're selling yourself and your future family short. Happiness isn't something you get because you've got things. Happiness comes from . . . well, from loving each other." She worked her jaw back and forth for a moment, as if gathering her thoughts, then continued. "I've known your brother, Philip, a long time — five years now — and he's been pretty open with me. So I'm going to make an observation based on what Philip's shared. Hold onto your hat."

Teasingly, Rocky put his hands on his head.

Eileen grinned and went on. "That desire of yours to give all kinds of extras, as you put it, comes from your misguided perception that *things* were what you lacked as a child. Rocky, it wasn't things; it was a feeling of belonging and affection. Your parents, for whatever reason, didn't know how to give that to you. But I know if they'd really made you feel loved, not getting a new bicycle or braces wouldn't have mattered a bit. I know, because that was my childhood. Never had more than two sets of clothes to my name, sure never got new toys, but I was never unhappy. Because my house burst at the seams with loving each other. I was so happy I never knew I was poor."

Rocky raised his eyebrows. He had a hard time believing her.

"Stop looking at me like that." She shook the blade of grass. "It's absolutely true. I had the love of my mama and daddy, and they taught me about the love of God, and that same God made sure every last one of my needs was met. I never once hungered for anything more than what I had. I was happy. Because I was loved."

"But times have changed," he argued.

Eileen sputtered, "Don't try telling me old values are outdated! They aren't! It's people that've changed, not the times. People have become dissatisfied with having their needs met and get all caught up in wants." She glowered at him. "You really think those rich people that live in East Briar are happy all the time? Bah! They're still people, Rocky, and people all need the same thing to make them happy — love. Love of God first, and love of family second."

She rolled to her feet and peered down at

156

him for a moment, her expression thoughtful. "Maybe you need to spend some time in prayer, young man. Ask God to get your priorities in alignment. And while you're at it, you might let God know you trust Him to meet your needs. He can do it. And while He's at it, He can give you the desires of your heart. But what you've got to remember is the biggest desire should always be to grow in your relationship with Him. That's where true happiness resides — in recognizing just how much He loves you."

She turned her back and returned to her digging. Rocky watched her for a few minutes, his thoughts tumbling haphazardly, sorting out what she'd said. He got to his feet and emptied the rest of the fertilizer in the spreader, but his mind wasn't on the task. He kept replaying what Eileen had said about God meeting his needs, God being the source of his happiness. He wanted to accept her words as fact, to set aside all the ideas of providing his family with the extras he'd mentioned, but a bit of doubt held him back.

What if Carrie's needs were different from most people's? After all, having grown up in a mansion, given all the extras money could buy, wouldn't those things that were wants to him have become needs to her? And how could he hope to provide those things for her with a simple landscaping business?

"Eileen?" He waited until she raised her head. "I'm going to put the spreader away; then I'll be back to help you put the rest of those mums in the ground. You okay out here by yourself?"

She waved a dirty glove in his direction. "Go on. I'm old, not helpless." As he started to walk away, she called, "And think about what I said! I'm not stupid, either."

He gave a nod in reply and rolled the spreader to the storage shed, cleaned it and put it away before heading back to assist Eileen in placing the remainder of the mums he had purchased. *Let God know you trust Him to meet your needs. . . .* Eileen's words repeated themselves in his memory. His heart pounded as fear struck. Maybe his faith wasn't strong enough for that yet. He had a lot of serious thinking and praying to do.

TWELVE

Carrie awakened before her alarm clock sounded, jolted from sleep by a troubling dream. She scowled into the dusky room, trying to pinpoint what had bothered her, but as was so often the case with dreams she was unable to recall the details that would bring understanding. With a sigh she rolled sideways and blinked the sleep from her eyes. A glance at the calendar hanging above her desk reminded her that in only six more days she would be twenty-five. And she would be independently wealthy.

She rolled the other way to avoid thinking about it.

Her contact with Rocky for the past three weeks had been nonexistent. Frustration built in her chest as she thought about it. She had known school would occupy her time during the weeks, but she had intended to see Rocky each weekend. Between her stepfather's interference and Rocky's com-

mitment to help his brother do some reno-
vating at his job placement service, she
hadn't seen him since their dissatisfying
picnic at the duck pond.

A sigh escaped. It hadn't seemed to matter much that she hadn't spent time with
Rocky in person. He was constantly present
in her thoughts. And her prayers. Despite
spending a portion of each day in prayer
concerning the roadblock that stood between her and Rocky, she hadn't found a
solution. No matter how she looked at it,
the trust fund would always be there.

She groaned and buried her face in her
pillows, petitioning heaven once more.
"How can You make this work, Lord? I love
Rocky, and I believe he loves me. Money
should never stand in the way of how people
feel about each other." She threw back the
covers and rose, padding to her desk and
tapping her finger thoughtfully on the date
that would change her life irrevocably.

Not only would she become responsible
for a large sum of money, Mac had informed
her she needed to find her own place to live.
"You've got the means to purchase a house.
I'll put you in touch with a realtor who can
assist you in making a wise choice," Mac
had said two nights ago at supper. At the
time Carrie had nearly fallen out of her seat

160

in surprise. She hadn't suspected Mac would throw her out of the only home she'd known since she was a very small girl. But now, thinking about it, it seemed like a good idea to go.

Purchasing a house and getting it ready for her habitation was a challenge in itself. Doing that while facing the starting rush of a taxing, final school year seemed daunting. But it also seemed exciting. She could make her own choices, decorate as she pleased — and she certainly had ideas for décor! Nothing flashy. She wanted homey, warm, and welcoming. Soft colors, durable furniture, and lots of flowers.

The thought of flowers brought her back to Rocky, and suddenly the dream that had awakened her drifted through her memory. Only a whisper of it, but enough to grasp the meaning. She'd dreamt she stood in the middle of a huge flower garden, with Rocky darting from cluster to cluster, his hands reaching, as if trying to decide which bloom to pick. She waited, holding her breath, for him to finally choose one, knowing it would be a flower with special significance; but finally he turned to her with great sorrow in his eyes. Holding out his hands in defeat, he said, "I'm sorry. I can't afford any of them." And instantly she'd awakened.

Now she jerked upright, an idea striking like a lightning bolt from the sky. So Rocky couldn't afford those flowers — *she* could! With her trust fund she could buy a field of flowers. But she didn't want a field of flowers already blooming; she wanted to buy the field in which to plant flowers, and a greenhouse, and tools and equipment needed to get a landscaping business on its feet. Remembering the sadness in the dream — Rocky's eyes when he was unable to gift her — was all the motivation she needed to start her plan in motion.

So Rocky couldn't afford to start his own business. All he needed was the capital. He'd asked her to pray for the means to make his dream a reality, and she'd overlooked the most obvious answer to the prayer — her very own trust fund. She wouldn't use it for herself; she'd use it for the good of others, starting with Rocky.

She dashed through a shower, dressed in a soft linen suit of beige, and pulled slingback pumps onto her feet. Back in the bathroom she twisted her still-damp hair into a coil on the back of her head and secured it well with pins then applied makeup with a careful hand. Just enough to bring out her cheekbones and enhance her already thick, full eyelashes. Taking a step back, she surveyed her reflection in the mirror. Satisfied, she marched out of the bathroom, snatched up her purse and keys, and headed for her car.

It was Saturday, and people would be busy, but they'd make time for Mac Steinwood's stepdaughter. A twinge of guilt struck as she realized she was doing exactly what she'd always disdained — using money to gain favors — but this favor wasn't for her. This was for the man she loved. It would be worth it.

Rocky rolled over in bed and stretched, yawning widely, as he forced his body to awaken. Normally on Saturdays he let himself sleep in since during the weekdays he was at work by five a.m. But today, as he had the past two Saturdays, he would be meeting Philip at New Beginnings to work on updating the training center.

He sat on the edge of the bed and rubbed his eyes. They should finish today — just touchup painting and putting everything back where it belonged. It had been a challenge for Philip to operate with things in a mess — many of his clients didn't adjust well to change, and the odd placement of partitions and furnishings had made things rather tense — but all would be in order by the end of this weekend.

And maybe, after this weekend, he could get his own life in order. While he'd worked with Philip, his thoughts often drifted to Carrie. It had been hard on his heart, not seeing her at all for twenty straight days. He hadn't called her, either. It didn't feel right to call the Steinwood mansion, so he'd waited for her to call him. But she hadn't. That bothered him. Maybe she'd decided a relationship with him wasn't a good idea after all.

He shook his head. He didn't want to think about that. What an unpleasant way to start a day. But he knew how to turn it around. Eyes still open, he prayed, "Dear God, thank You for this day and the chance to do some good work. Be with me as I help Philip finish up at New Beginnings. Be with Carrie, whatever she's doing. Bless her time and protect her. Let us both bring glory to You today. Amen."

The prayer made his heart feel light. Rising, he entered the bathroom and ran a washcloth over his face, scrubbing away the remainder of sleepiness. He gave his whiskery chin a quick shave, pulled on a clean pair of jeans and a T-shirt, then locked up the house and headed to New Beginnings.

Philip was already there, as was his wife,

Marin, and Marin's brother, John. He greeted Philip with a clap on the back, gave Marin a hug and a kiss on the cheek, then turned to John.

"Good morning, John." Rocky kept his hands at his sides. Even though nearly a dozen years had passed since his youth, when he had tormented John and others like him, the guilt of his former behavior still plagued him when he saw John.

John's almond eyes crinkled into a smile as he replied, "Good morning, Rocky. Today we are finishing so things will be neat and tidy." His stubby hands signed the words as he spoke.

"Neat and tidy sounds good to me," Rocky agreed then hesitantly gave John a light pat on the shoulder.

John didn't shrink away, just slung his arm around Rocky's back and patted, too. How forgiving John was. Rocky wished he could be as accepting as John was of others.

"Well, let's get going," Philip said. "Paint cans and brushes are over there. Be sure to lay out the plastic sheet before you get started. I don't want paint spatters on my new floor."

"Okay, okay, tyrant." Rocky forced a grumbling tone as he grinned at his brother and headed toward the paint.

John shook his head. "Rocky, this is not tyrant. This is Philip. You do not remember your brother?"

Philip laughed lightly. "He remembers, John. He's just teasing me."

John laughed, too. "Oh, he is teasing. Okay." Then he shook his finger at Rocky. "But no more teasing. Teasing is not nice."

Another pang of guilt struck. John was right — often teasing hurt. John would know. He saluted. "No more teasing."

They all got busy. Philip cranked up his radio on a Christian music station, and the soul-stirring songs inspired Rocky as he worked. He hummed along with the tunes, mouthing the words occasionally, while his paint brush swished in beat with the music. He heard the phrase "Jesus makes all things new . . ." come through the speaker, and it reminded him of the verse in Second Corinthians that had captured his attention a few nights ago during his reading.

He paused, the paintbrush still, as he tried to recapture the exact wording from his Bible. In a whisper he recited, " 'Therefore if any man be in Christ, he is a new creature: old things are passed away; behold, all things are become new.' " He was pretty sure he got it word for word. He said it to himself again, absorbing the meaning of the words.

Dipping the brush once more, he reflected on old things passing away. He glanced over his shoulder to spot John with his shoulder against a partition, pushing while Philip guided it into place. John's face creased in concentration, his tongue showing in the corner of his mouth, made Rocky smile.

Who would have thought Rocky Wilder would spend time with a man with Down Syndrome? The old Rocky wouldn't have, except to torment him, but the new Rocky was finding an admiration for people with disabilities. Despite any shortcomings perceived by society, John continued to do his best with what he'd been given. Everyone should be as friendly, accepting, and diligent as John.

" 'All things are become new . . .' " Rocky whispered the words as he stroked paint onto the wall. New. Shiny. Rocky hadn't owned very many new, shiny things in his lifetime. His folks had shopped garage sales and donation sites for clothes and toys. His first car had been fifteen years old when he'd bought it, all the new worn off. Hard to take something like that, buff it up, and make it appear new.

Not so with a man's heart, though, he

thought with a rush of joy. When God got hold of a person, He didn't just blow off the dust, sandblast the rust, then polish it to hide the old worn-out parts. God replaced the old parts with brand-new, shiny parts. He made things *new.*

Rocky glanced once more at John. "God, I sure wish I could go back and change the mean things I did," he whispered, his heart aching as he thought of the pain he'd caused. "But thank You for the opportunity to be John's friend now. I hope I can keep things shiny in my relationship with him."

He turned back to the wall, examined his handiwork then stooped to touch up a scuff mark near the baseboard. The swish of paint eradicated the mar, giving the entire wall a new appearance. He smiled, satisfied with his work. Suddenly, against the backdrop of pale beige, Carrie's image appeared. Fresh, clean, honest. How did that verse in Second Corinthians apply to people like Carrie, whose lives had been lived with everything shiny and new?

The telephone jangled. Philip answered it then called, "Hey, Rocky? It's for you."

For me? Rocky trotted to the phone, took the receiver with two fingers and pressed it to his ear. "This is Rocky."

"Hi, Rocky, it's Carrie."

Carrie! His knees turned to jelly. Bracing himself on the edge of Philip's desk, he squeaked out, "Hi. How'd you find me here?"

A soft laugh came through the line, causing Rocky's heart to double its tempo. "I've called all over Petersburg, it seems. You weren't home, your brother wasn't home, so I finally called Eileen, and she told me where you were. Oh — she said to tell you she'll bring lunch over for all of you."

"Thanks," he said. "But —"

"And speaking of food . . ." Did he hear hesitance in her voice? "You know I've got a birthday around the corner. I'd like you to have dinner with my parents and me to celebrate. Can you come?"

A lump formed in his throat. Dinner in the Steinwood mansion? There wasn't enough polish in the world to shine him up enough to match that place. But how could he refuse? "I'd enjoy that. Thanks for asking."

"Good." She told him the day and time then added, her voice tender, "And don't be nervous. Just be yourself. That's good enough."

The lump nearly strangled him. How he loved this woman. He swallowed hard. "Thanks, Carrie. I'll see you then."

■ ■ ■ ■

Carrie hung up the phone then leaned back in her desk chair, satisfied. She'd had a productive morning. In front of her were the forms used in filing for a new business, a list of probable expenses related to starting said business, paperwork from the bank to transfer funds from her account to Rocky's as it was needed to cover startup expenses, and donation forms from the college to establish a scholarship for his use.

Her fingers trembled as she stacked the papers and slid them into a folder marked simply "for Rocky." It pleased her that the money left by her father could be put to use for good. She suspected Rocky's pride might make him balk at first, but she hoped she could persuade him to accept this gift in the manner intended. She wanted it to convey her belief in his abilities. Everything had fallen so neatly into place this morning that she couldn't help but believe it was God's will for Rocky to start his business, and it gave her great joy to be part of the answer to his prayer.

While out, she had also stopped by a realtor's office and requested a listing of all available single-dwelling houses in town.

The agent who greeted her had been only too eager to show her the most ostentatious, costliest houses on the market. He'd looked at her as if she'd lost her mind when she indicated she wanted a modest home, but he had given her the information she wanted. She knew she needed to look right away — Mac seemed eager to have her out on her own — yet she felt uneasy choosing a house by herself.

It wasn't as if she didn't know what to look for. Mac was in the business of constructing quality houses and businesses. She'd grown up watching, listening, learning. So she could choose a house that was structurally sound. What she wanted was someone at her side who would see the house from the viewpoint of its becoming a home.

She wanted Rocky to help her. But would he? She thought of his trailer house — its lack of pretension. He'd seemed embarrassed by its simplicity, and her heart had ached when he'd apologized for it. If she asked him to help her choose a home for herself, would he be able to do so without feeling second-best? She wanted to build Rocky up, not intimidate him.

Sighing, she tucked the folder into a drawer in her desk, out of the sight of prying eyes. She'd just have to do some more praying, ask God to open Rocky's heart to understand her intentions. Because, if she had her way, Rocky would be a permanent fixture in her life from here on out.

THIRTEEN

Rocky pulled up to the curb outside the Steinwood mansion and turned off the ignition. He sat for a minute, his heart thudding painfully, as he gathered the courage needed to get out of the car. He looked up and down the street — no other vehicles in sight. Had the other guests pulled into the drive and parked behind the house? A large garage and expanse of concrete provided a parking area back there. Should he do the same? Then he shook his head — no, his older model car would look ridiculous next to the cars driven by the no doubt wealthy guests waiting inside.

Carrie waited inside, too.

He drew in a great breath then released it slowly, an attempt to calm his ragged nerves. "Get out and go into the house," he mumbled. With a trembling hand he pulled the door release and stepped onto the street. Standing beside his car, he took a moment to tighten the knot on his tie and straighten the lapels of his new jacket. He resisted the urge to run his hand through his hair. The new shorter cut, styled only that morning, felt alien to his fingers.

Pushing his keys into his pocket, he forced his feet to move to the iron gates that had intrigued him as a child. He paused beside the keyboard, wondering what to do, then he saw a button marked "intercom." With one finger he pressed it then leaned forward to listen.

"Yes?" came a voice — female and formal.

He straightened. "Yes, I —." His dry throat made his voice sound croaky, so he swallowed and tried again. "I'm here for Carrie's birthday dinner."

"Name, please?"

Rocky shoved his hands into his pockets. "Rocky Wilder."

Not even a pause before the instruction came. "You will hear a buzz; then the gates will open. You will have fifteen seconds to proceed through before the gates begin to close."

"Thank you."

The words were barely out of his mouth when the buzzer sounded. Rocky didn't waste any time stepping through. He was halfway up the brick driveway before the gates reversed themselves and sealed him inside. As the gates clicked, he stopped and turned back to look. As a kid, how often had he imagined what it would feel like to be on the inside looking out?

The gates were the same from both directions — scrolled, black iron with a solid oval in the center bearing the gold letter *S* for Steinwood. When he was young, he thought he'd feel different, special, to be allowed inside the sacred ground of the Steinwood mansion. But for some reason now, realizing he was stuck in here until someone let him out, he only felt trapped. A chill crept up his spine.

Giving himself a shake, he turned and went the remainder of the way to the porch. He stepped past deeply cushioned white wicker furniture and potted plants and crossed to the double doors that would allow him access to his childhood dream house. As he raised his hand to press the brass doorbell, the door swung open, and Carrie caught him with his finger pointed in midair.

Her smile made his insides spin like the blade on a power mower. "Hi, Rocky. I'm so glad you made it. Come on in."

She moved aside, allowing him entry, and he stepped over the threshold to root himself on the marble floor of a two-story foyer. Although curiosity made him want to gawk at everything, see if it was all the way he'd imagined, he kept his gaze on her. It wasn't too difficult to focus on her, though — she was beautiful in a flowing dress of white scattered all over with roses. He allowed his gaze to rove from her tumbling blond curls to the bright pink sandals on her feet, and he whistled softly.

"Wow, Carrie, you look . . . wonderful." He couldn't find a word good enough to describe her.

She laughed, touching one curl that fell across her shoulder. "Thank you. So do you." Her slender hand took hold of the tip of his tie, lifted it and let it fall, much the way she had at the park. "I like this — is it new?"

Rocky cupped his fingers around the tie and ran them down its length. "Tie's not, but the jacket is." He leaned forward and whispered, "Am I dressed okay? I didn't want to — you know — stick out."

Her tender smile touched him deeply. "You're perfect, Rocky. Quit worrying."

"And I didn't bring you a present. I . . ." He faltered. To be honest, he hadn't known what he could buy that she didn't already have. He should have picked up some flowers — maybe a bouquet of pink roses. Those would coordinate perfectly with her appearance this evening.

"Just coming this evening is present enough," she assured him. Then she put her hands on her hips and gave a mock scowl. "But what did you do to your hair?"

He chuckled ruefully as he touched the cropped strands above his left ear. "Got it all styled for you. Some lady named Diana did it. What do you think?"

Carrie leaned sideways, a teasing grin on her face, and thoroughly examined his new haircut. Finally she shook her head. "It looks nice, Rocky, but it'll take some getting used to. I sure liked those curls along your collar. I've always been tempted to give one a tweak."

His brows shot upward. She had wanted to tweak the curls at his collar? Her words must have surprised her as much as they had him because her face suddenly flooded with pink that matched the roses on her dress. His own grin grew broad as he teased, "So now the truth comes out."

Assuming a stern expression, she pointed a finger at him. "Yes, well, don't let it go to your head. Especially now that it's impossible — no curls in sight."

He nodded, his grin still stretching his cheeks.

"Carrie? Are you going to introduce your guest?"

The deep voice from behind them startled their gazes apart. Carrie took him by the elbow and turned him toward a man Rocky immediately recognized — Mackenzie Steinwood. The last time he'd seen Steinwood was in juvenile court, when the man had testified against him. Back then, although tall for his age, Rocky had been the shorter of the pair. Now he towered over Steinwood by at least three inches.

The man had aged — graying hair was combed straight back from his high forehead, and lines around his jowls gave him a stern appearance. But he twisted his face into the semblance of a smile as Carrie made the introductions.

"Mac, this is Rocky Wilder. Rocky, this is my stepfather, Mac Steinwood."

Rocky held out his hand, and Steinwood took it, the man's palm soft against Rocky's calluses. "It's nice to meet you, sir."

"Well, it's hardly a first meeting, is it?" The man's sardonic voice let Rocky know exactly where he stood. "We have met before, although these circumstances are certainly more pleasant."

Rocky wasn't sure how to respond. Before he could form an answer, Carrie gave his elbow a tug.

"I know Myrna has things ready for us. Let's go to the dining room, shall we?" She guided him past Steinwood, through a wide doorway and across highly polished floors scattered with thick, patterned rugs, to what was clearly the formal dining room. Rocky kept his gaze straight ahead, aware of Steinwood behind him. He felt certain the man watched his every move.

An older version of Carrie stepped into the room from a door on the opposite wall just as they entered the dining room. Although Rocky could see beauty in the woman's delicate features, a hardness in her eyes distracted him. She crossed immediately to Rocky and offered her hand. It was so thin Rocky was afraid to touch it.

"Good evening. Mr. Wilder, is that correct? Carrie has spoken so highly of you. I'm her mother, Lynette. I'm pleased to make your acquaintance."

"Thank you, ma'am." Rocky gingerly clasped the woman's hand, considering her words. Though welcoming in content, the lack of warmth in the delivery gave him a chill. He glanced over his shoulder to find Steinwood fixing him with a distrusting glare. There was no question — Rocky did not belong here. He had a sudden desire to excuse himself, head right back to the double doors, and go home.

"Rocky?" Carrie sensed the tension in Rocky's frame. She wished she could give both of her parents a good tongue-lashing for making him feel so uncomfortable. It certainly wasn't hospitable! But it would have to wait until later. The important thing to do now was make Rocky feel at home.

She waited until he glanced down at her — even in her three-inch heels, he still stood inches taller than her. She loved the feeling of protection his height offered. "Let me show you to your seat." She guided him to the table which was set for four.

His gaze bounced from the table to her face. "Just the four of us?" His voice rasped out in a whisper meant only for her ears.

"Yes." She leaned closer, her shoulder against the firm muscle of his upper arm. "That's what I wanted. You'll be fine." She gave his arm a reassuring squeeze as she smiled into his face. Then, raising her voice, she said, "You sit here, next to me."

He pleased her by pulling out her chair before seating himself. By the time they were settled, Mac had seated Lynette, and she rang a little bell to signal Myrna to bring in the first course.

Stilted conversation carried them through the appetizer of French onion soup and the main course of chicken breasts smothered in grilled mushrooms, onions and peppers, served with wild rice and steamed baby carrots. As the birthday girl, Carrie had been allowed to choose the menu. She'd selected her favorites, but she hardly tasted the food, keenly aware of Rocky's discomfort. And Mac wasn't helping that one bit! Her anger stirred as Mac set his fork aside and pinned Rocky with a look that could only be described as challenging.

"So, Mr. Wilder" — the disdainful tone set Carrie's teeth on edge — "tell me how you've occupied your time since last we talked."

Carrie watched Rocky fold his hands together, his fingers so tightly linked his knuckles looked white. He cleared his throat, his Adam's apple bobbing. She longed to put her hand on his knee, offer some support, but she was afraid to move.

"Well, sir, as you know, after our last meeting I spent some time in a detention center. It wasn't exactly summer camp." He managed a light, self-deprecating chuckle. "But it served its purpose — made me determined to straighten myself out."

"So can I assume you did straighten yourself out?"

Carrie wanted to give her stepfather a kick under the table. Since when were guests treated so rudely? But Mac was sending her a clear message — Rocky wasn't considered a guest but an intrusion in his home.

"Yes, for the most part. I never stole anything again." Rocky offered a shrug, the navy blue jacket pulling tight across his broad shoulders with the movement. "Doesn't mean I was perfect, but I was better."

"So you finished school?"

"Yes, sir. Graduated from high school."

"And what college curriculum did you choose?"

Carrie bit down on the end of her tongue. Mac was being deliberately cruel!

Rocky had every reason to rail at the man, but his mild answer made her chest expand in pride. "I haven't had the privilege of college . . . yet."

Mac perked up at the subtly dangled bait. "Yet?"

At that moment Myrna bustled in to remove dinner plates and ask Carrie if she was ready for her cake. Carrie nodded, relieved by the distraction the dessert would provide. She went through the formality of blowing out the candles, although the birthday song went unsung. Myrna cut and served huge squares of the decorated confection then disappeared back into the kitchen.

The moment the door swung shut behind the cook, Mac picked up the dropped topic. "Can I presume you intend to begin a study at college?"

Rocky put down his fork, swallowed the bite in his mouth and swiped his napkin across his lips before answering. "Yes, sir. I do hope to attend college. I plan on opening a landscaping business."

Mac leaned back, raising his eyebrows high in a look of feigned interest. "Landscaping? Well, I believe Petersburg has one landscaper at work now. Have you investigated the need for a second?"

Carrie's gaze flitted back and forth between the two men as the conversation moved quickly.

"Yes, sir. I believe there's enough work, with all the new construction going on right now, to support two landscaping businesses in town."

"And our local university provides the necessary course work?"

"Courses in both science and business. I

could get everything I need right here."

"You would continue working at Elmwood Towers while attending school? Or do you plan to quit work altogether and focus on college?"

"Frankly I can't afford to quit. I'll have to take as many evening classes as possible so I can keep my job."

"Mm-hm. . . ." Mac crossed his hands over his chest and fixed Rocky with a penetrating look. "Evening classes. It will probably take twice as long to finish that way. That would mean you'd be — what? Thirty-five? Thirty-six years old when you finish?"

Mac's cruelty made Carrie's heart ache. Must Rocky be knocked down at every turn? She opened her mouth to defend her friend, but Rocky spoke first.

"I realize it'll take me longer. I realize I'm late getting started." His quiet, respectful tone pleased Carrie. "But God planted this dream, He gave me the ability to do the job well, and I trust I'm doing what He's planned for me. I trust Him to help me make it all happen."

Mac waved his hand, his expression contemptuous. "God is fine for old women and children, but men —"

"Men are wise to recognize their need for

184

their Creator," Rocky interrupted softly. Although tension showed in the lines around his eyes, he faced Mac without rancor and continued. "I thought it would be a sign of weakness, too, to give myself over to God, but when I accepted the gift of salvation through His Son's sacrifice at Calvary, I suddenly realized how wrong I was. My own strength was nothing compared to God's strength in me. I don't know how I made it as long as I did without Him."

Carrie felt tears behind her lids. Nothing proved God's presence in Rocky's heart more than his calm rebuttal to Mac's intentional goading. Love and admiration welled up within her, and she looked Rocky full in the face, praying he'd recognize the light of approval in her eyes.

He met her gaze, and the soft smile he offered let her know he appreciated her silent support. Suddenly he rose. "Thank you for inviting me here this evening. I've enjoyed myself. And, Mrs. Steinwood" — he swung his gaze toward Carrie's mother — "please tell your cook everything was delicious. But" — he turned back to Carrie — "it's getting late, and I don't want to wear out my welcome."

Although Carrie was disappointed he wanted to leave so soon, she understood.

Why would he want to spend any more time visiting with Mac? She rose, too, taking hold of his elbow. "I'll walk you out."

They walked without speaking until they reached the gates, which Carrie opened. Then they paused on the drive with the gates spread around them like a giant pair of wings.

"I'm sorry Mac was rude." Her heart ached at the way Rocky had been treated.

He offered a shrug. "I don't blame him. His memories of me aren't too great."

Carrie would have admired him less had he spoken disparagingly. His refusal to berate Mac spoke clearly of God's influence. She wrapped her arms around his neck and gave him a hug. "Thank you for coming, Rocky."

His firm arms came around her briefly; then he stepped back, pushing his hands into his pockets. "Thank you for inviting me. I–I'd better go."

She watched him drive away, waving until his car turned the corner; then she looked back toward the house. Squaring her shoulders, she prepared for a storm. She marched to the house, stomped directly to the dining room and wheeled on her stepfather.

"Of all the rude, uncivilized ways to treat someone." It gave her satisfaction to see

Mac pull the coffee cup away from his lips and lift his startled gaze to her. "Rocky was a guest in your home, but you treated him like an intruder. What were you doing?"

"Carrie, darling," her mother said, lifting her hand toward Carrie.

Carrie shook her head. "It's too late, Mother. You said nothing the whole time he was here, which was just as reprehensible as Mac's attempts at intimidation. Neither of you treated him well. He was my guest — my only guest. Was it too much to ask you to be polite?"

Mac rose to his feet, glowering. "Yes, as a matter of fact, it was. He doesn't belong in this house. That Wilder boy is a common thief and a delinquent. He'll never amount to anything, and I hope this evening proved to you just how ridiculous your association with him is."

Carrie met her stepfather's angry gaze without flinching. "All this evening proved was how much Rocky has changed since he was a boy. The old Rocky would have risen to your bait, gotten angry, said things that were unkind. But he didn't, did he? He was respectful even when you weren't. 'That Wilder boy,' as you call him, no longer exists, Mac. He's a new creation with Christ in his heart, and I love him."

"Love." Mac released a snort of derision. "You're insane."

"No, I don't believe so. But I won't spend time debating that with you. I will tell you this, however — I intend to support Rocky in his business venture. I believe in his talent and ability, and I am going to do whatever I can to make his dream a reality."

"Well, that explains why he would spend time with you — for what he can get," Mac said in a derogatory tone. He thrust out his chin. "But what can he possibly give in return?"

Mac's question, though thrown out in anger, made Carrie take a step back. She offered an honest reply. "All I want from him is his love and respect. That's the greatest thing one human being can give another."

"Bah!" Mac spun toward the door. His back toward her, he grated out, "You're a fool, Carrie. Love and respect won't pay bills. You'll waste your money on that piece of trash, and he'll leave you high and dry. I just hope that God of yours will be able to pick up the pieces." He stormed out of the room.

Carrie turned to her mother. "Is that how you feel, too?" Lynette dropped her gaze to the tabletop. "Mac is rarely wrong, Carrie."

Carrie could have argued that, but she knew it was pointless. It saddened her that her parents were so close-minded. The acquisition of money and prestige had become their god. Their hearts were hardened to anything else. She released a sigh. "I'm sorry you feel that way, Mom, because what I told Mac is true. I love Rocky, and I will help him, even if you disapprove."

Her mother stood slowly, as if very tired, and crossed to Carrie. She touched Carrie's cheek and offered a weary smile. "You're an adult, darling, and you don't need our approval to spend the money your father left you. But —" She bit down on her lip, and whatever she'd intended to say went unsaid. She gave her head a little shake. "I must go see to Mac now." She walked out, leaving Carrie alone.

Carrie closed her eyes and whispered a prayer. "I'm so sorry I've upset them, God, but they're wrong. What I'm doing for Rocky is the right thing to do. Please help them see that, and let them somehow find their way to You."

FOURTEEN

A sense of relief washed over Rocky as he drove away from the Steinwood mansion. Who would have guessed that spending time in that house — that beautiful, flashy, made-of-dreams house — would leave him feeling so cold? Now, remembering how he had fantasized about the house as a child, he felt foolish. He turned his vehicle toward his own humble home, realizing the people living in the Steinwood mansion were no happier than the ones who had lived in his old neighborhood. In fact, they might even be less happy.

Mrs. Steinwood had sat silent through the entire dinner, picking at the delicious foods on her plate rather than eating. In her silk pantsuit and tastefully chosen jewelry she was stunningly attired, but she had reminded him of a decorated skeleton — there seemed to be no life inside the shell of her body.

And then there was Mr. Steinwood. He clearly didn't trust Rocky. While Rocky understood that, he suspected Steinwood didn't trust anybody. He lived in fear of someone taking away the things he owned. Instead of finding pleasure in his wealth, the wealth had made him bitter, jealous, and suspicious. Rocky shook his head. He sure didn't ever want to be like that. Maybe being wealthy wasn't such a great thing after all.

Eileen had told him having his needs met was enough. At the time he'd wondered if she could possibly be right. Now he understood what she meant. Having too much changed a person, and from what he'd just seen of the Steinwoods it didn't change someone for the better.

He paused at a traffic light, a sudden thought striking him. What of Carrie? Would her sudden acquisition of the trust fund change her, too? *Lord, don't let it spoil her,* he prayed inwardly. *Don't let it make her bitter and distrustful, the way it has Steinwood. . . .*

He turned onto the final stretch that would lead him home. If he were going to have his needs met with his own business, he'd better get things going. He'd made some preliminary inquiries already, but he hadn't done anything official to make the business happen. Monday he'd see if he could take the afternoon off. That would free him to go to the licensing bureau and start paperwork. He'd also visit his sister-in-law Marin at Brooks Advertising, find out what she could do for him, then stop by the college and pick up an application.

There was much to do, and Rocky was eager to get it going.

"I'd love to work with you on this, Rocky." Marin's enthusiastic tone made Rocky even more excited about his new business venture. "You know Philip and I will do anything we can to help you get this started."

"Thanks." He hadn't expected anything less from Marin, but he wanted to be sure he wasn't putting her in an awkward position. "I know Jefferson Landscaping is already one of your clients. It's okay to take care of my business, too, since we're both landscapers?"

She smiled, her eyes crinkling slightly. "Not to worry. We design the advertising campaign; we don't personally endorse our clients, so there's no breach of confidence here." She leaned back in her chair and winked. "Since you're family, though, it might be tempting to endorse you."

Rocky laughed. "Don't get yourself in trouble." Cupping his chin, he posed a hesitant question. "If I get this going . . . do you think . . . John might be interested in working with me?"

Marin's eyebrows shot upward. "John?"

Rocky nodded. "Yes. He's helped Eileen with several garden plots at Elmwood Towers and seems to enjoy working in the soil."

"And you'd really consider hiring him?"

Rocky understood the surprise in Marin's voice. "I know how I used to be about people who are different, but as I've gotten to know John . . ." He shrugged. "I like him. He's a neat guy."

She smiled. "I think so, too." She paused for a moment, nibbling her lower lip. "I would have no problem with him working with you, but he really likes his job at the veterinary clinic." Marin's tone sounded thoughtful. "I suppose, once you have things started, we could ask him if he'd like to change jobs. And if not John, perhaps another of Philip's clients?"

Rocky nodded. "Sure. That'd be fine. I'll mention it to Philip." He stood up. "Thanks, Marin. When I get everything going I'll be back, and we can talk about how I'll pay for your services."

Marin rose, too, and walked him out of

the office. "Let's worry about that later. You're family — I have special rates for family."

Rocky gave Marin a quick hug then headed back to his car. College applications for admission and financial assistance waited on the passenger side of the seat. He fingered the papers as he drove to the licensing bureau. He felt a little overwhelmed by all the paperwork — the lady in the financial aid office had said things must be filled out accurately in order to be processed. What if he made mistakes? Maybe he'd ask Philip to help him with that. After all, Philip had already gone through college.

Rocky felt a pang of regret. His little brother was miles ahead of him when it came to establishing his future — he had a college degree, owned his own business, which offered help to people with handicaps, and was married. Rocky, the older brother, was only getting started. Was is too late, like Mac Steinwood had said? Then he shook his head. No, it was never too late to do the right thing. Determination straightened his spine. He'd see this through.

He parked in front of the licensing bureau then headed inside. A middle-aged receptionist greeted him. "Hello," he responded. "I'd like to find out what I need to do to get a new business started in town."

She flashed a smile. "Certainly! You've got to get city approval, fill out tax documents, and file an application with the business bureau." She turned toward a file and began removing forms, making a stack on the corner of the counter. "What kind of business are you planning to start?"

Rocky leaned his elbows on the counter. "Landscaping."

"Landscaping, hm?" The woman paused, releasing a light chuckle. "There seems to be a lot of that going around lately."

Foreboding made the hair on Rocky's neck prickle. "Oh yeah?"

"Yes. Someone was in here a few days ago talking about starting a new landscaping business."

Rocky stood up straight. "Who was it?"

The woman shrugged. "I'm not at liberty to say. She just mentioned the paperwork was for a landscaping venture."

She? Rocky's heart pounded. A sick feeling struck his stomach.

The receptionist took one more form from the drawer, added it to the stack then placed everything in a large manila envelope bearing the business bureau's mailing address. "You can send everything back in this same envelope," she said.

"Thank you." Rocky pursed his lips for a moment. "You're sure this other person was interested in a landscaping business?"

"Oh yes, I'm sure." With another bright smile she said, "Now don't let that bother you. Competition is good for businesses." She handed him the envelope. "Good luck with yours."

"Thank you." He stepped out of the office into the afternoon sunshine. He stood for a moment outside the door, tapping his leg with the envelope, his thoughts racing. Could it have been Carrie getting information about a landscaping business? Rocky had heard of Mac Steinwood undercutting others to get the best profit. If he had his own landscaping company, he wouldn't need to rely on someone else to landscape the grounds of the businesses and houses he built. Maybe, now that Steinwood knew Rocky's plans, he had convinced Carrie to get a family landscaping business going first. After all, Carrie had her business administration degree, so she had the training, not to mention the financial means, to get a business started.

But surely Carrie wouldn't . . . He shook his head. No, Carrie wouldn't do that to him. She knew how much this business meant to him. But, his thoughts countered, she'd grown up with Mac Steinwood. He was the only father she'd had for most of her life. Her loyalty to Steinwood would certainly be deeper than any loyalty to Rocky.

He slapped his leg with the envelope and charged to his car. He didn't want to think ill of Carrie. He'd go see her, talk to her, and let her laugh and tell him how silly he was for even thinking such a thing. It would be okay, he told himself as he drove once more to the Steinwood mansion. Everything would be okay.

Carrie turned the corner, and her heart skipped a beat when she saw Rocky's car parked along the curb. Getting to see him twice in three days after their lengthy separation was almost too good to be true. She pulled into the driveway but didn't open the gates — instead she popped the car into park, bounced out leaving the door hanging open and crossed to meet him as he stepped onto the asphalt road.

"Hi!" She felt lighter just seeing him. It had been a stressful day of labs and exams, and time with Rocky seemed the perfect antidote to stress. "What are you doing here?"

He didn't smile in return. "I came to see you."

She rested her weight on one foot and tipped her head, offering a smirk. "Well, from the look on your face your day hasn't been much better than mine. How long have you been waiting?"

He glanced at his watch. "Since around four."

"Four!" She couldn't believe he'd been sitting out there for more than two hours. "Why didn't you just call?"

His shoulders lifted in a shrug. She waited for him to make a teasing remark about her being worth the wait. When none came, trepidation struck. "It must be important then. Do you want to go inside?"

Rocky shook his head, his gaze flitting toward the closed gates. "No. Not really. Can — can we just sit in my car and talk?"

"Sure." She backed toward her own vehicle. "Let me shut off my engine. I'll be back." She trotted to her car, her heart pounding. Something was wrong. Dreadfully wrong. She prayed for God's strength as she twisted the key in the ignition, closed her door, then joined Rocky.

He had to shift aside an envelope as she slid in. She recognized the address on the label — the business bureau. She hoped he hadn't gotten bad news about using the land he'd purchased to start a landscaping business.

Forcing a cheerful tone, she asked, "So what's up?"

Rocky rested his elbow on the steering wheel, his finger across his lips. He stared out the window for a few seconds before turning to face her. "I just wondered if you might know something about another landscape business starting up in town."

Carrie processed her best response to his question. If she told him what she was up to, it would spoil the surprise. Also, based on his mood, he might outright reject her assistance. She didn't want to face either prospect. Yet she couldn't lie to him. So she asked carefully, "Do you mean one other than the one you're planning to start?"

"That's right."

She could reply honestly to that. "No, I don't. Why do you ask?"

Rocky drew in a big breath. He tapped the envelope on the seat between them. "I went in today to get information about how to apply to start a new business, and I was told a woman was in a few days ago, asking about the same type of business. It . . . worried me, I guess."

"Afraid of a little healthy competition?"

she teased, praying he wouldn't out-and-out ask if she were the woman.

"Not at all," Rocky replied, his expression serious. "Competition is fine. I just want to be sure I stand a chance of making the business work. After all, Petersburg isn't exactly a metropolis. It can certainly support two landscaping businesses with all the new construction going on here and in surrounding communities, but three? It would be pretty foolhardy to think that many would stand a chance of succeeding."

Carrie gave a slow nod. "You might be right."

He twisted his face into a scowl. "With Jefferson Landscaping already well established, I'm taking a risk, coming in new. I sure hope there isn't another one." He gave her a sharp look. "You're sure you don't know of a third one?"

Carrie laughed. "Rocky!" She hoped she sounded convincing. "I told you I don't know about a third one." She needed to get this conversation turned. Although she had intended to wait until he started college to tell him about a computer program she'd found, she decided this might be a good way to get him focused on something else.

"But I do know something that might be of use to you."

"Oh yeah?" He didn't sound terribly interested, but at least he asked. "What's that?"

"A landscaping program for the computer." She shifted in the seat, angling herself toward him. "It's amazing. You can put in the geographic location of the area being landscaped, and the computer makes suggestions for types of plants that grow well in that area. It even breaks it down between leafy versus flowering plants, and shade-lovers versus sun-lovers, and everything in between. Then, if you put in the dimensions of the garden area — four feet by ten feet, for instance — it offers some blueprints of plots you can follow."

Rocky gave her a funny look. "I don't know how to use the computer, Carrie."

He certainly was a gloomy Gus today! She patted his knee. "You'll learn. It really isn't that hard. And this program —"

"I like planning it myself."

She frowned at his argumentative tone. "Well, you still could do the planning if you wanted to and just use the program to determine what kinds of plants to use."

He looked at her for several long seconds, his expression unreadable. Finally he said, "I suppose you're right." His gaze drifted out the window again.

She huffed in annoyance. "Rocky, couldn't you at least be a little enthusiastic? I mean, here you are, preparing to open your very own business, and this program could be a great help. Why not at least consider using it?"

He turned to face her, his brows pulled down into a worried look. "How do you know about this program, Carrie? Why were you even looking for programs related to landscaping?"

His apprehensive tone bothered her. She flipped her hands outward in a gesture of inquiry. "Didn't you ask me to pray for your business and to help? I look at different programs for one of my classes. I found this one, and I thought of you."

He nodded, his gaze never wavering from hers. "Oh. Well . . . thanks. But . . . as I said before, I don't know how to use computers."

She shook her head. He had no idea how easy it would be to use these computer programs. She gave his knee another encouraging pat and said, "It's okay, Rocky. I know how."

Now she was sure he looked worried. And shamed. She reached to touch his arm, but he twisted to face forward, reaching for the ignition. "Thanks, Carrie. I'll — I'll look into that program, okay? I'll bet you've got studying to do, right? I won't keep you from it." He glanced briefly in her direction, his eyes tired. "Will you be at Bible study Wednesday?"

For some reason she fought tears. "Yes. Shall we sit together?"

"That would be fine." His voice sounded tight, controlled.

She put her hand on the door handle, ready to leave, then spun toward him. "Rocky?"

"Yeah?"

"I —" But then she clamped her jaw shut. If she told him now about filing the application and setting up a scholarship, she would be ruining a wonderful surprise. She didn't want to do that. Although he was worried now, he'd understand everything later. She shook her head. "Nothing. Never mind. I'll see you Wednesday."

She stepped out of the vehicle, leaned forward to wave good-bye then closed the door. Watching him drive away, she felt a little twinge of anxiety. But she pushed it aside. When Rocky learned the truth, he'd be too excited to care about her evasiveness. A smile grew on her face — besides that, she'd have another way to distract him by Wednesday. She'd know by then whether the house she bid on would be hers.

Hopping back in her car, she punched in the code for the gates, started the engine, and headed for the garage. She couldn't wait to tell Myrna about her new soon-to-be home.

FIFTEEN

Rocky slammed through his front door, giving it a kick with his heel to bang it closed. He threw himself onto the couch, his head back and eyes closed, hurt pressing so hard he feared his heart might stop beating.

He didn't like to think of it, but Carrie had lied to him. He'd been around enough liars in his lifetime to recognize untruths when they were spoken. She hadn't been able to meet his eyes, her laugh had been too high-pitched to be real, and her tone too cheery. It all pointed to one thing — she wasn't being honest.

She was hiding something, and since all the issue-skirting pertained to the information about another landscaping business, he knew it had to do with that. She was in up to her eyeballs. But why shouldn't she be? She had the know-how to start a business, she had the finances to get it going, she had the connections through her stepfather —

everything for success was already in her hand. Born with a silver spoon in her mouth, the old saying went. And now she was waving it, ready to use it to her advantage.

The wealthy just get wealthier, he thought, a bitter taste on his tongue, *while the rest of us get shoved aside.* It burned like a fire in his gut to have Carrie be the one to do the shoving, but he really couldn't blame her. She had witnessed her stepfather shoving people aside for years — it must be second nature to her by now.

His nose stung, a sure sign he wanted to cry. But what would that help? His father had told him tears were a waste of energy, and for once Pop had been right — tears accomplished nothing. *Focus on something else,* he told himself. Supper. Get something to eat. Fill up the emptiness in his belly.

Bolting to his feet, he stomped to the kitchen and flung the refrigerator door open. Not much in there — he needed to go grocery shopping. He whacked the door shut and started swinging cupboard doors open and closed. With a huff he considered his choices for supper — cold cereal or canned ravioli. Yuk on both counts.

Leaning against the counter, he shook his head, his shoulders slumped. Why had he set himself up this way? Hadn't he told himself from the beginning that being with Carrie was a mistake? They were from two different worlds. She had tried — she had honestly tried — but the tug of the Steinwoods was too strong. They'd reeled her back. He'd hoped . . . His nose stung again. But, no, it was foolhardy to hope for a relationship with someone like Carrie.

"Oh, Lord, I just wish it didn't hurt so much."

At least he had his relationship with his Father God. The Bible study lessons came back to him — how God was always there, would never forsake him. An old-fashioned word, forsake, but Rocky liked it. It meant God was totally dependable — he didn't have to worry that God would abandon him. God would never let the search for money or prestige get in the way of His relationship with His child Rocky. A feeling of comfort wrapped around Rocky's aching heart.

He dropped to his knees in the kitchen and poured out his hurt to God. Then he prayed for Carrie, for her happiness. "Let her discover the key to happiness isn't in gaining more money, God. Don't let her turn out like her parents — she's just too good for a life like that." It helped to pray for her, and he remembered the biblical advice to pray for those who persecuted you. He'd always thought that odd — why pray for someone who wanted to harm you? Yet praying for Carrie brought a great sense of peace.

He got to his feet, remembering the picnic lunch he'd shared with her. That day she had nearly convinced him her money didn't mean anything to her — that it shouldn't come between them. She had listened so intently to his dreams, had told him God loved him the way he was and had encouraged him to pursue opening his landscaping business. He pushed his hands deep into his pockets, his shoulders stiff, as confusion struck. Why would she do all that if she was just going to turn around and undermine him? It didn't make sense.

And standing there, staring off into space, didn't make sense either. Carrie had made her choice. He'd have to accept it. Reaching for his phone, he made his plans for the evening. He'd order a pizza, watch some TV then fill out all that paperwork so he could get it in the mail. Just once the Steinwoods were going to come in second. Rocky would play their game of hardball, and he would win.

■ ■ ■ ■

Wednesday evening Carrie sat on a metal folding chair in the church basement and fumed. Rocky had done it again. The last time he'd left her sitting alone was in the pizza parlor, and she'd wondered what happened to him. This time she knew what happened — he was running scared. Again.

There'd been something in his eyes Monday when he'd stopped by the house. The old worry was back about how he could compete with the Steinwood money. How she wished he'd set that silliness aside and just accept her for who she was! She was willing to accept him, warts and all. Couldn't he do the same for her?

She got very little out of the Bible study with thoughts of Rocky distracting her, and her college classes Thursday weren't much better. On Thursday evening, when the realtor called to tell her she could stop by and sign paperwork for her new home on Friday, she hung up in excitement and immediately began to dial Rocky's number. Then remembrance struck again, and she slammed down the phone in frustration. By Friday morning, when she still felt tense and annoyed, she knew she'd have to hash things out with him.

She got out of class a little after one and, instead of going to the realtor's office, headed for Elmwood Towers. Walking toward the courtyard, she encountered Rocky's white-haired friend, Eileen, who greeted her with a huge smile.

"Why, hello! I bet you're here to see Rocky."

Carrie forced her lips into a smile. "Yes, I am. Do you know where I might find him?"

Eileen nodded, her eyes crinkling. "Oh yes, I do. He's placing some rocks in the flower garden we started a few weeks ago — he decided it needed some texture." She winked. "And *you* might be just what *he* needs. He's been a real grumble-bear this week." Eileen pointed. "Just follow the foot path. You'll see him."

Carrie thanked Eileen and headed down the foot path she and Rocky had taken on that afternoon when she had boldly asked him to spend some time with her. She spotted him, in his ratty sleeveless T-shirt and worn denims, and the sight of his flexing biceps and tanned skin immediately made her stomach turn a flip-flop. The effect this man had on her senses. . . .

"Rocky." She called his name when she was still several yards away.

He turned, a sizable rock in his hand, and his gaze narrowed. He waited until she stood in front of him before asking, "What are you doing here? Don't you have class?"

"I get out early on Fridays. And speaking of class . . . where were you Wednesday night?"

He turned back to the garden, bending over to place the rock between a middle-sized bush and a cluster of something that must have bloomed at one time but now was flowerless. He took his time, shifting the rock just so, then straightened and brushed his gloved palms against each other to dispel dust.

"I was busy."

She tipped her head, frowning. "Well, you might have let me know. I held a seat for you, and you didn't show up."

"I'm sorry." But his tone didn't sound sorry.

Carrie's ire raised. "Listen, Rocky — after you stood me up at the Ironstone, you said you wouldn't do that again. And then you did do it again. Is this going to be a habit?"

He jerked off his gloves, throwing them into the wheelbarrow. Then he stuck his fingertips into his pockets and looked at her. His brown eyes, normally warm and welcoming toward her, seemed cold and distant. She felt a chill.

He drawled, "I guess . . . habits . . . are hard for all of us to break."

Her scowl deepened, and she put her hand on her hip. "What is that supposed to mean?"

"Nothing." He turned back to the wheelbarrow, reaching for his gloves.

She grabbed his arm and tugged, forcing him to look at her. "Rocky, we're beyond this. Don't shut me out. I had some news I wanted to share with you Wednesday, and when you weren't there it really disappointed me. The least you can do is tell me why you didn't come."

He looked into her eyes for a long moment, his face puckered up in — what? Frustration? Confusion? She wasn't sure. Finally he gave a shrug and said, "Okay, I'll tell you why I didn't come. I couldn't stop thinking about that woman who got information about starting a landscaping business. I couldn't stop thinking that, even though you tried to hide it, it was you. You're not a very good liar, Carrie."

She felt a blush climbing her cheeks.

"See — you're getting all pink. You lied to me Monday. Are you going to lie to me now and say it wasn't you who picked up those applications?"

He had her trapped. She couldn't look him in the face and tell an outright fabrication. She shook her head miserably. "No. It was me."

"That's what I thought." He snatched up his gloves and jammed his hands in, adjusting the fingers, his lips set in a grim line. Then he lifted a rock, grunting with the effort of clearing the side of the wheelbarrow. He took two stumbling steps forward and thumped the rock down. Still leaning forward, hands on knees, he added in a tired voice, "And I just couldn't sit there next to you, knowing what you'd done."

Carrie felt her heart plummet. He'd known all along. There never was a surprise. Disappointment hit hard — she had so wanted to surprise him. "You mean you *know* what I was doing?"

He pushed himself upright and faced her, his expression hard. "Of course I do. It's clear. Your stepfather builds things. All of those buildings are on unlandscaped ground. It only makes sense that having a landscaper in the family would be to his benefit." He rubbed the back of his neck, grimacing. "Of course it smarted to think you'd be the one to start it, since you knew how much I wanted to get my own business going; but from a business standpoint I —"

213

"Wait a minute." Carrie took a step forward, one ear turned toward him in an effort to hear more clearly. "You think I picked up that paperwork so I could start my own landscaping business — one that would be in direct competition with yours?"

He threw his arms outward. "What else was I to think? I'm not stupid, even if I don't have a college degree. You've got everything it takes — knowledge in business administration, the skills to get whatever you need right off the computer, the money to hire workers and make it all happen." He snorted. "Your whole life you've watched Mac Steinwood find ways to add to his bank account."

Suddenly he seemed to deflate, shaking his head and looking toward the ground. "Look, Carrie — I understand. Sure, it hurt, but . . . I do understand. It's the way you were raised. I don't blame you."

She stood, staring in disbelief, the ache so intense it nearly doubled her over. He thought she was working against him instead of for him. He thought her upbringing as Mac Steinwood's stepdaughter would make her stoop low enough to pull the rug out from under the feet of someone she genuinely cared about. Tears clouded her vision, and she took a step backward. He was like everyone else, only seeing her money, not seeing her heart. She had thought Rocky was different, but he wasn't. She choked back a sob.

His head came up, his gaze locking on hers. "Carrie, don't cry. I told you it didn't matter."

"Oh, but it does." Her voice quavered with the effort of maintaining control of her emotions. "It matters a great deal. And if that's what you really think of me, then —" She shook her head, another sob nearly strangling her. Should she tell him why she picked up that paperwork? No — he wouldn't believe her. And she couldn't face more of his rejection.

"I–I've got to go. Good-bye, Rocky." The last two words nearly broke her heart. She spun on her heel and clattered down the sidewalk, determined to escape. But how would she escape this pain in her heart?

Rocky sat on the metal step in front of his trailer, a bottle of pop in his hand and a heavy weight in his heart. He'd made Carrie cry today. As upset and hurt as he'd been, he hadn't wanted to do that. Seeing her distress had created a whole new hurt inside of him. Why should he care if he'd upset her after what she'd done? He knew why. Because he loved her.

He rubbed the sweaty bottle across his forehead, trying to cool his thoughts. Yep, he loved her all right. But what good did that do him? She'd come right out and admitted the truth — that she had picked up the paperwork for a landscaping business. But her parting comment — something about if that's what he thought of her — kept plaguing him. If she were guilty of plotting against him, why would she assume he'd feel anything but bitterness? It didn't make sense.

He released a breath, his cheeks puffed out, then looked across his acre of ground. In his mind he could still see the little green stems pushing their way through the soil, the seedlings stretching toward the sky. It was a good dream. One he wasn't willing to relinquish. Eileen had told him God planted the talent in him, and he needed to let that talent bloom. How ugly would a rose bush be without the blooms? That's how he felt now, having someone try to steal his dream away — like a prickly rose bush stem with no blossoms.

Carrie's stricken face appeared again in his memory. He heard her words again — "If that's what you think of me" — and he scowled. He wished he could set that memory aside. He didn't want to think of her right now. It hurt too much.

Swallowing the last of the carbonated beverage, he gave the bottle a toss to the Dumpster at the edge of the yard. It smacked the rim and bounced out. Immediately he got to his feet, strode across the ground, snatched up the bottle, and dropped it in. As the bottle thudded in the bottom of the barrel, he couldn't help chuckling. Who would have imagined it — Rocky Wilder, worrying about trash on the ground? God sure had worked a change in him.

So why couldn't God work a change in Carrie, too?

The thought struck hard. His heart pounded. He'd broken his habits of apathy and intimidation. If God could help him set aside those lifelong traits, couldn't He also help Carrie set aside her lifelong lessons of putting money first?

A Bible verse about it being harder for a wealthy man to enter the kingdom of heaven than it was for a camel to pass through the eye of a needle flitted through his mind. He raised his eyes to the sky, now tinged with pink, and asked aloud, "You said it was hard, God. But is it impossible?"

He didn't receive an answer. He didn't

even feel any peace. With a sinking heart he turned toward the trailer door. His feet scuffed through the dirt as he crossed the yard. Maybe he'd better focus on something else. All this nervous energy should be put to good use, and he'd use it all right. He'd use it getting his landscaping business going. Now. His brother would be able to help. First thing tomorrow he'd see Philip, get his advice.

"And I won't even think about Carrie," he told himself firmly.

But his thoughts added disparagingly, *Yeah, right.*

Sixteen

"Okay, I think that's a pretty comprehensive list." Philip tapped his pencil against the yellow writing pad on the kitchen table.

Rocky glanced at the pad, his resolve faltering as he took in the lengthy list of things to do. Then he straightened his spine and said, "It's a lot, but I'll do it. I'll leave Steinwood in the dust."

Philip's forehead creased into a scowl. "Rocky, I think it's great that you want to open your own business. And you know Marin and I will do anything we can to help."

Rocky met Philip's gaze, his lips twisting into a wry grin. "I hear a 'but' coming on."

Philip shrugged, grimacing. "But . . . I'm worried about the hostility I hear in your voice. You seem more interested in outdoing Steinwood than anything else. That doesn't seem healthy to me."

Rocky shifted his gaze to the kitchen

window. The morning sun backlit the yellow gingham curtains, making them glow with cheeriness. The curtains reminded Rocky of daffodils nodding their heads on a spring morning. Everything reminded him of flowers — landscaping seemed to be in his blood. He wanted this business so badly he could taste it.

"Is it wrong to want to be successful?" he asked, his gaze still on the window.

"Of course not." Philip's firm tone brought Rocky's gaze around. "But at the expense of someone else's failure?"

Rocky gritted his teeth. "Look — you and I both know Steinwood won't be a failure. He'll get business — his own. But I'm determined to get everyone else's, whatever that might take." He leaned back and folded his arms across his chest, his throat constricting. "He has this coming. He and Carrie cooked up this scheme to start their own business just so I wouldn't stand a chance. Steinwood hates me — I stole from him. He doesn't want me to be successful. So he used a weapon I couldn't fight against — Carrie — to bring me to my knees. Well, it isn't going to work. I'm going to be successful, and they're going to have to swallow their pride and acknowledge that they lost."

Philip shook his head. "Listen to yourself, Rocky. Now you're even turning on Carrie."

Rocky felt pressure build in his chest. He clenched his fists. "I don't have a choice! She turned on me first!"

"Are you sure?"

Philip's calm question stirred Rocky's anger. "Of course I'm sure. She admitted it."

"She admitted picking up paperwork for a landscaping business. She didn't admit to trying to put you out of business."

Rocky snorted in disgust. "They're one and the same."

"Are they? How can you be sure?"

Rocky pushed his chair backward, lurching to his feet and stomping across the linoleum floor to lean against the kitchen counter and peer out the window. Philip's questions had brought a niggle of doubt to Rocky's mind. He didn't want to believe ill of Carrie — he really wanted to believe she hadn't intended him harm. But he didn't know how to balance her confession of guilt against what he felt in his heart.

"I'm just a sucker for a pretty face." His quiet admission was tinged with self-deprecation.

Philip rose and stood beside him, resting

his hand on Rocky's shoulder. "I can't tell you what to do — never could — you were always so stubborn."

Rocky managed a slight smile at those words.

"But I'd like to give you a word of advice."

Rocky turned his head to look at his brother.

"If you care about this girl as much as I think you do, don't let it go like this. The bitterness will eat you alive. Talk it out. *Work* it out."

"I don't think we can," Rocky said, shaking his head. "We're so different."

"I thought the same thing about Marin and me," Philip pointed out. "We had a huge stumbling block to overcome — a seemingly insurmountable issue that had to be forgiven. I didn't think it was possible either, but look at us now. With God all things are possible. Don't underestimate Him, Rocky."

Rocky considered Philip's words. Was it possible for him to forgive Carrie for this act of sabotage? Would they be able to bridge the differences in their upbringings and find a common ground? It seemed overwhelming. He blew out a breath of frustration. "I don't know. . . ."

"You don't have to know," Philip said, giving Rocky a firm clap on the shoulder. "You just have to trust. But I hope you'll make the effort, because if you don't, you'll always wonder what could have been. And that's a regret I can't imagine you'd want to carry for the rest of your life."

"Put it right over there against the north wall."

Carrie directed the movers in the placement of her couch. The plastic covering crinkled as the two men pushed the overstuffed couch into place. She smiled her thanks, but before she could voice the words a ringing intruded. Her cell phone, which was in her purse. But where was her purse?

She dashed around the room, peeking behind boxes and stubbing her toe before she located the leather bag squashed between two boxes on the kitchen counter. Standing on one foot, she flipped the phone open and panted, "Hello?"

"Miss Mays?"

"Yes."

"This is Vicki at the university financial aid office. I was calling to let you know the scholarship fund you requested is available now. We'll hold the paperwork for Mr. Wilder. Do you want to notify him, or would you prefer we sent him a letter?"

Carrie's heart began to pound at the mention of Rocky's name. She hadn't spoken to Rocky in two weeks — not since that day when he'd accused her of intending to put him out of business.

"Um," she hedged, rubbing her throbbing toe. "I guess send him a letter."

"That's fine," the woman chirped. "We can give him all the instructions for enrollment at the same time."

"Yes, that would be good." Carrie wouldn't have to do anything — just slink away and let Rocky take care of himself. Her heart ached more than her toe.

"Do you have his mailing address?"

Carrie dug through her purse for the little address book she kept with her calendar and recited Rocky's address. Then she disconnected the call, her duty done. She plopped the phone back into her purse, leaning her head on her hand for a moment as regret washed over her.

How differently she'd envisioned all this when she planned it. Taking Rocky to the college, seeing his face light up when he realized schooling was paid for, telling him how God had prompted her to use her money to answer his prayers.

But the misunderstanding had changed all that. His accusations still stung, and she didn't know if she could ever face him again. Surely when he got the letter he'd understand what she had tried to do, but even if he apologized, would she be able to forget the hurtful things he'd said about her?

With a sigh, she limped through the kitchen doorway back to the living room where the movers deposited the country-style hutch for her dining room. She glanced around. That was the last of the furniture she'd purchased — their job was done. Retrieving her purse, she tipped them generously for their help and saw them out.

She stood in the doorway of her new home, watching through the full-length glass storm door as the moving truck pulled away from the curb and growled down the street. The silence of the house pressed around her. Loneliness struck. She whispered, "God, I feel very alone right now. Remind me of Your presence, please?"

Turning from the window, she searched for the box which contained her stereo and CDs. She finally located it, shoved some things aside on the floor to uncover an outlet, and soon the room shook with music from a Christian male band. Carrie sang along, her doldrums lifting as the music reminded her she was never alone.

An hour later she had her kitchen cupboards in order and a pile of empty boxes to carry out. She stacked the boxes together and placed them in the garage out of sight. As she stepped back inside, the words "Jesus only speaks the truth" rang out on the CD. Carrie paused, listening as the song ran its course.

She wished Rocky would listen to the truth instead of believing she had lied to him. It hurt so much, having him turn on her that way. Stepping out of comfort zones was something both she and Rocky would have to do if they were to make their relationship work. They'd have to meet somewhere in the middle. She'd already taken the first step, moving out of the Steinwood mansion to live on her own. But Rocky would have to make the bigger step — accepting her money without allowing it to trample his pride.

She imagined him receiving the letter from the college, reading the invitation to enroll, seeing the financial sheet marked "paid in full." In her mind's eye she envisioned two scenarios — the first, him socking the air in joy and shouting a thank-you for the opportunity; the second, wadding up the letter and throwing it away, angry that someone had interfered.

She sighed, defeated. The second scenario

seemed much more realistic based on her last encounter with him. Rocky wouldn't accept it. His pride wouldn't allow him to accept it. What had she been thinking? She should never have forged forward with this ridiculous scheme. Her heart had been in the right place, but she should have thought it through.

She reached for her purse and removed her phone. A quick call to the college could divert that scholarship to some other needy student. Then she wouldn't have to worry about Rocky Wilder and his oversized sense of pride.

But she stood, finger poised over the keypad, while something held her back. Even as much as he had hurt her with his misplaced accusation, she wanted him to have this advantage. He'd had few advantages growing up. Surely he deserved this one. She closed the phone and pushed it slowly back into her purse, her thoughts tumbling.

She would leave the decision in his hands. If he rejected it, then she would ask the college to give it to someone else. But before he could reject it he'd have to know the motivation behind the gift. She needed to talk to him just once more. The thought of him believing she would deliberately sabotage him was a thought with which she could no longer live. He'd face the truth no matter what it took.

Should she invite him here? She considered that. She wanted him to see her house, to show him she had moved out of the Steinwood mansion and was no longer a part of that world. Yet she sensed she needed to meet him on his court. No, she wouldn't invite him here. He might not come. But she could go to him, and she would. One more surprise for Rocky — a surprise visit — and she'd at least have the opportunity to defend herself. If he still chose to believe the worst, then she would accept it. But she had to try just once more. She cared too much to let it go.

Rocky closed his Bible and leaned back. Guilt pressed at him. The last verse of the fourth chapter of James weighed heavily on his heart. If a person knew to do good and didn't do it, it was sin. And sin, Rocky knew, grieved his Father.

He'd been wrong to accuse Carrie, to hold himself aloof. She was his Christian sister, and even if she had behaved inappropriately he'd been wrong, too, to harbor anger against her. One sin was as bad as another in God's eyes — Rocky knew that.

"What do I do, God? How do I make it right?" He spoke the words aloud. The first time he'd wronged Carrie, it had been a simple matter to fix it — flowers and a book. But this wrong was far different from accidentally spraying her with water. This wrong had been deliberate. He'd purposely avoided her, purposely accused her, purposely hurt her. This couldn't be fixed with a handful of impatiens and a used romance novel.

Drawing in a deep breath, he considered his options. He could ignore the situation and hope it would stop bothering him. He shook his head — the guilty feelings wouldn't go away. Philip had even said he might regret it for the rest of his life, always wondering what might have been. Ignoring it wasn't an option.

He tapped his lower lip with one finger. Well, then, he could write her a letter, apologize in writing and hope she accepted it. But that didn't seem right, either. Besides, his writing wasn't all that great. It would be embarrassing to have someone as smart as Carrie trying to figure out his chicken scratchings and misspelled words.

He ran his fingers through his hair, releasing a huff of breath. The only other thing he could think of was to talk to her. By telephone? He snorted and berated himself. "Quit trying to take the coward's way out." No, he'd have to talk to her in person. He broke out in a cold sweat as he thought about pushing that intercom button at the Steinwood mansion's gates and asking to speak to Carrie. But there was no other way. And the sooner he got it done, the better it would be.

He slammed the footrest down on the recliner and stomped, barefooted, to his bedroom. He changed into a clean pair of jeans and a shirt that had sleeves, making sure he tucked in the tails neatly. He dug under his bed for a pair of socks that weren't too dirty and his tennis shoes. He tied the laces extra tight, frustrated by the quiver in his hands. After running a comb through his hair and splashing on some aftershave, he felt ready to face Carrie.

The drive to the Steinwood mansion took a little over fifteen minutes. Fifteen minutes of battling his nerves. By the time he reached the gates, his hand trembled like a leaf in a hurricane. But he managed to get his finger to connect with the intercom button.

"Yes?" A female voice. He surmised by the warm tone it did not belong to Mrs. Steinwood. It must be Myrna.

"Yes . . . um, I'd like to speak to Carrie?"

"I'm sorry, sir," the voice came, "but Miss Carrie no longer resides here."

Rocky drew back, stunned. "She doesn't?"

"No, sir. She's —"

"Who is this?" A new voice intruded, masculine and demanding. Mac Steinwood.

Rocky swallowed hard. "This is Rocky Wilder, Mr. Steinwood. I'm looking for Carrie."

"She moved out. And I assured her I would allow *her* the privilege of sharing her new address with others. Have a good day, Mr. Wilder." A click indicated the intercom had been disconnected.

Rocky leaned back and ran his hand through his hair. Now what? How would he find her? If she'd requested her new address be kept private, then she didn't want to see or hear from him. Regret struck. Philip was right — he should have taken care of this days ago.

With his shoulders slumped in defeat, Rocky shifted his car into reverse, backed out of the driveway and turned toward home. The drive seemed to stretch forever as the weight of guilt pressed on him. "Help me, Lord. I don't know what to do. Please — somehow bring Carrie to me."

A quarter mile from his house, the sight

of a car waiting in his yard set his heart to pounding so hard he feared it might break free of his chest. A little red sports car. "Heavenly Father, is it — ?" It was. It was Carrie's car. And Carrie waited in the driver's seat.

SEVENTEEN

Even as she stepped out of her car and watched him pull into the drive, Rocky still had a hard time believing she was really there. He'd just prayed for her to come to him, and — *boom!* — there she was. He didn't know prayers could be answered so quickly.

He shut off his ignition and shot out of his vehicle, closing the distance between them in less than a half-dozen long strides. "Carrie?" He heard the disbelief in his own voice. "What are you doing here?"

"I came to see you." She sounded subdued, hesitant. Not that he could blame her. "Can we talk?"

"Yeah. Sure. Let's — let's go inside, huh?" He gestured toward the door, and she followed him up the metal steps and through his front door. Inside, she hovered on the square of linoleum that served as his foyer area, her hands clasped in front of her. How uncomfortable she appeared.

"Go ahead and sit down," he encouraged. "Can I get you something to drink? I've got a cola in the fridge, or some ice water."

"No, nothing, thanks." She seated herself on the edge of the couch, resting her hands in her lap.

Her blue-eyed gaze followed him as he moved to his recliner and sat. He wrapped his fingers around the armrest of the chair and met her gaze. Neither spoke for several long, tense seconds. Then he heard a chuckle rumble from his own chest. "This is so . . . weird."

She tipped her head, her blond hair spilling across her shoulder. "What is?"

"I just came from the Steinwood mansion. I went to talk to you, but your stepfather said you'd moved out."

"Yes. Once I got my trust fund, Mac said I should be on my own."

Trust fund. Rocky's gut clenched with those words. A reminder of their vast differences. "He wouldn't tell me where you lived now." There was a hint of accusation in his tone. He hadn't intended it, but it was there — leftover resentment.

Her chin shot up, a stubborn thrust to the line of her jaw. "I planned to tell you about my new house that night at church, but you didn't come." Her tone matched his in accusation.

He cleared his throat and made the apology he had planned. "That was wrong of me, Carrie. Will you forgive me?"

Her gaze lowered for a moment. "Actually, Rocky, your not showing up hurt a lot less than the reason you didn't come."

Hurt welled up in Rocky's chest. Hurt for her duplicity. Hurt for the discomfort he had caused her. One hurt was for himself, the other for her, and he couldn't decide which one took precedence. "I'm sorry about that, but I couldn't face you. Not knowing . . . what I knew."

She met his gaze squarely. "But that's just it. You didn't know. You made an assumption, but it was incorrect. That's why I came here tonight. You need to know the truth."

Rocky pushed himself firmly against the backrest of the recliner. The chair squeaked. "What is the truth, Carrie?"

She leaned forward, resting her elbows on her knees and fixing him with a fervent look. "The truth is I picked up that paperwork for you. I wanted to help you. I knew how to get things rolling, and I thought if I could start it all, it would simplify things for you."

He shook his head, unsure he understood. "You were trying to get *my* business started?"

She grimaced. "You sound as if I were trying to take it over."

"I didn't mean it that way." But, he wondered, what did he mean? If Carrie had done all that for him, was it because she didn't think he was capable of handling it on his own, or was she really trying to be supportive? Old insecurities made him want to believe the former. "I'm curious why you'd do that."

She sat up, raising her shoulders in a graceful shrug. "I care about you, Rocky. You wanted it so badly. You'd asked me to pray about your landscaping business. When I prayed, it occurred to me that I could be a real help. So I pressed forward, thinking I would surprise you by getting some of the paperwork out of the way. But" — her gaze dropped to her hands where she fit her fingertips together, forming a steeple — "you found out and jumped to a conclusion, and . . ."

When she didn't finish her thought, Rocky completed it for her. "And you couldn't tell me because you were afraid I wouldn't listen." Philip had been right. Regret was hard to carry.

A slight nod confirmed his guess. "You were so cold that day. I didn't know how to fix things. So I left." Cupping her hands over her knees, she said, "But I couldn't leave that disagreement between us. I wanted you at least to know the truth. So I had to come."

He leaned forward and captured one of her hands. "I'm glad you came, Carrie. And I'm so sorry I hurt you that way." He shook his head. "I should have known." Swallowing the lump of regret, he confided, "Growing up, I didn't find many people I could trust. I guess, as much as I'm trying not to be that Wilder boy who carries a chip on his shoulder, sometimes he still makes an appearance. I shouldn't have jumped to conclusions."

"I can see why you thought what you did," she said, surprising him with her understanding. She pursed her lips for a moment, a hesitance coming across her expression. "And actually I haven't told you everything yet."

He held his breath, waiting.

"In addition to picking up paperwork at the business bureau, I also set up a fund for you at the college. All you have to do is go in and enroll. Your expenses are covered."

He leaned back, releasing her hand. A pressure built in his chest, and words burst out. "I can't let you do that."

"Why not?"

"It — it's too much. College is expensive."

"I can afford it."

"That's not the point!" He shot out of his seat and paced across the room. Desire and defiance mingled in his chest. How he wanted this degree. He'd prayed for it, asked for God to provide the funds, but how could he take Carrie's money? There would be no way he could repay her. "I can't — I can't take something I didn't earn."

A soft laugh escaped her lips. "Really? Then why did you accept salvation? Or are you telling me you earned that?"

He spun around. "That's not the same thing."

She rose and crossed to him. "I know. Salvation is a much bigger gift than anything I could offer." She took his hand. "Rocky, what I'm offering comes with no strings attached. You asked me to pray for you, and God laid it on my heart to help you. If you truly don't want to use the fund I set up for you, then I'll give it to someone else. But I'd prefer you used it."

He stood in silence, her slender fingers cool against his palm, while he battled mixed emotions. A part of him wanted this opportunity. A part of him balked at the idea of taking money from her. Despite himself he released a throaty chuckle. Rocky Wilder was trying to avoid taking something from someone? Who would have guessed it?

"Look, Rocky — all you have to do is swallow your pride and the money is yours. You have a gift — you can bring beauty to the world. Accept the fund, get your degree, start your business, and use that gift for others. It's only as difficult as you choose to make it."

He drew in a deep breath then released it slowly. He reached out, pulling her into his arms. The scent of apples filled his nostrils as he rested his chin on her hair. "This is tough, you know? I'm not used to people being so nice to me."

She laughed and pulled free. "Well, get used to it. Because I can see me being even nicer."

He raised his eyebrows. "Oh yeah? How so?"

"Well . . ." She moved a few feet away, her hair swaying across her back. "I've got my business degree, too, you know. And I've always liked the idea of starting my own business rather than working for someone else. What's to say we couldn't combine forces? With your talent and my business acumen it would surely be a raving success."

He couldn't stop the grin that grew on his

cheek. Combining forces with Carrie sounded better than anything he could have imagined. "That sounds pretty good." He crossed his arms and smirked at her. "I like the idea of Wilder and Mays Landscaping."

"Wilder and Mays?" She quirked her brow, her expression teasing. "Haven't you ever heard of alphabetical order?"

He laughed.

"Or that a lady precedes a gentleman?"

He laughed louder. How had he managed to get along for even so brief a time without her? "You're too much, Carrie."

"I hope not." All teasing was set aside. "I hope . . . nothing about me is too much."

He knew she referred to her wealth. He closed the gap between them, taking hold of her hands. "I'm sorry I've let your money come between us. It's awkward, you know? As the man I feel like I need to be the stronger one in all areas, including financial."

She lifted her gaze, tears twinkling in the corners of her eyes. "I know, Rocky, but I can't make it go away. I come as a package — me . . . and my money. I can't tell you how hard I've prayed for someone to be able to accept me for myself and not want me because I'm wealthy. You're the first person who has rejected me because I was wealthy.

That didn't hurt any less."

Rocky wished he could kiss her pain away. But he remained still, her hands in his, as she continued.

"I know when you look at me, there's a part of you that sees my stepfather. But, Rocky, I don't want to be like Mac. I don't want to hoard this money. I don't want to use it to control people or impress people. I've got it, and I can't change that, but I can choose to use it for good."

Rocky, looking into her shimmering eyes, saw how much his false accusation had cost her. Before he could apologize again, she went on.

"I bought a house, and I bought some things to go in it. I think my father would approve of that. But for the most part I want to give the money away. Your college fund is the first of many scholarships I want to give to people who might otherwise not be able to get an education. I'm setting up an account with the college for that.

"I also want to donate a sum to your brother's business — I really admire what he does in the community for our members with handicaps. And I know there will be other charity organizations that can benefit."

"You — you're going to give it away?"

■ ■ ■ ■

Carrie heard the astonishment in Rocky's tone, and for a moment she faltered. Was he disappointed? Had he finally decided having her *and* her money would be a good thing? Her heart pounded as she answered, "Yes. I have no desire to live the lifestyle of my parents. I want simplicity, Rocky. Does — does that make a difference?"

He released her hands and took a step back, his eyes wide. Running his hand through his hair, he shook his head. "I'm just amazed, that's all. I mean, you could do anything you wanted to with your money. Travel, buy a house on the beach, send your kids to the best private schools. Why not do that?"

"Because I've seen how money changes people. It makes them greedy and suspicious, and they start thinking they're worth more because their bank account is bigger. Oh, I'm sure not all wealthy people are like that, but the ones I've grown up around?" She shook her head. "I don't want to be like that. I don't want the money to turn me into someone unlikable."

Rocky grinned. "Like that could happen."

She refused to find humor in the situation. "It could, Rocky. I saw it happen with my own mother. I believe she loved Daddy, but after he died she didn't go looking for love — she went looking for money. She'd become so accustomed to moving in the highest social circle that she couldn't accept anything less. She married Mac, and I'm not sure she's ever been happy." She sighed, her heart aching. "That old saying about money can't buy happiness is sure true — I've seen the evidence in my own house-hold."

Rocky didn't say anything, just stood with his gaze angled toward the picture window.

"Are — are you disappointed?"

Suddenly he seemed to come to life. Turning toward her, he shook his head, a smile lighting his face. "You are amazing, Carrie. The most unselfish person I've ever . . ." He dropped his gaze for a moment, as if gathering his thoughts. Finally he raised his chin, meeting her gaze. "I don't want your money, Carrie. I never did. It . . . unsettled me. I knew I couldn't compete with it." Taking a step closer, his expression turned serious. "You aren't giving it away to satisfy me, are you? You're doing this because you really want to, not because you feel pressured?"

Warmth flooded Carrie's middle. As much as her money intimidated him, he didn't want her to part with it to satisfy him. He cared for her — her, Carrie — so much that he was willing to accept the money if it was what she wanted. The knowledge made her feel light as air.

"I don't feel pressured. I want to use it for others' good."

He nodded, approval shining in his eyes. "Good. That's really good."

"And you'll accept the college fund?" She held her breath, hoping.

Although he hesitated, at last he gave a slight nod. "Yes. I'll accept it." His voice turned husky as he added, "Thank you, Carrie."

"You're welcome."

They stood without speaking, gazes locked, while Carrie wished he would lean forward and kiss her. But instead of leaning toward her he suddenly rocked back on his heels and clapped his palms together.

"So . . . you bought a house, huh?"

She blinked twice in surprise at this sudden change in topics. "Yes. Yes, I did." She took two hesitant steps in his direction. "Would you like to see it?"

"Sure!"

His enthusiasm brought a smile to her face. "It's still pretty messy — boxes everywhere. I haven't had time to put everything away yet."

"I could help with that, if you like."

She gave a nod. "I'd like that."

He crossed his arms and frowned down at her. "How's the yard landscaped?"

She sighed. "It's nothing to brag about. One big maple in the front yard, and another in the back, as well as what I think is a Russian thistle — at least it's covered with seed pods that look like little Christmas ornaments. But shrubs and flowers? Nothing. It's almost a clean slate."

He grinned. "Betcha I can help with that, too."

She laughed. "I just bet you can." Smirking, she added, "The first project for Mays and Wilder."

He pointed his finger at her. "That's Wilder and Mays, young lady."

She raised one eyebrow and didn't respond.

"Or perhaps we could try something else."

Carrie tipped her head. "Like?"

"Like . . . Wilder and Wilder."

EIGHTEEN

Carrie angled her gaze to observe Rocky as they headed toward the college. How at ease he appeared, leaning back in the driver's seat, his wrist slung over the steering wheel, the other arm propped on the window opening. He had a cat-who-swallowed-the-canary look about him, and his handsomeness, as always, made her heart thrum in her chest.

He whisked a glance in her direction, his face breaking into a smile. "Whatcha looking at over there?"

"You."

"Oh yeah?" He chuckled, his gaze on the road. "Can't imagine that would hold your attention for too long."

She resisted giving him a bop on the arm. "Don't underestimate yourself, Rocky. You have to remember you're no longer *just* Rocky Wilder — you're a child of the King. Tell yourself that each time you look in the mirror."

He gave her a smile that sent her heart *ka-wump*ing. Taking hold of the steering wheel with his left hand, he reached across the seat with his right and clasped her fingers. "Thanks, Carrie. Sometimes I'm just . . . overwhelmed, I guess . . . that you see me that way. You're so good and so —"

She squeezed his fingers. "Hold it right there. I'm not any better than you, so don't go in that direction. We're all sinners saved by grace, Rocky. I'm no better and no worse than you. We're both new creatures in Christ. That makes us even, okay?"

Another smile thanked her for her words. He released her to put both hands on the steering wheel and guide the car into a parking space. But as they headed across the sidewalk toward the administration building he took hold of her hand again, and this time he held tight until they reached the financial aid office.

Carrie reluctantly released his hand — it felt so good, so secure, to have her hand within his broad, strong fingers — so he could pick up a pen and sign the paperwork that would officially enroll him for the spring semester.

As he filled in boxes with black ink, she raised on tiptoes and whispered, "I can help you with your homework, if you'd like."

His lips twitched into a grin. "You sayin' I won't be able to handle myself in these classes?"

A shake of her head denied his statement. "Not at all. Just making myself available."

The grin deepened, bringing out the dimples she loved. "Hmm . . . might need you *every* evening. Sure you're up to that?"

She saw the teasing glint in his eye, but something else lingered there, too. She'd seen it the night at his house when he'd dropped the idea of calling their business Wilder and Wilder. A longing, perhaps, coupled with a hesitance.

She pressed her shoulder to his upper arm. Using a deliberately light tone she said, "For you, I could make the sacrifice of every evening." Her heart thudded — what might he say next?

But he didn't reply, just gave her a wink and returned to his paperwork. Carrie remained silent, too, allowing him to concentrate, but underneath her calm exterior her thoughts tumbled. Was he trying to gather his courage and ask her something important? Or was he merely teasing? How she wished he would get to the point!

Finally Rocky signed the last document and handed it to the secretary.

"Welcome to Petersburg University," the woman said.

Rocky nodded in the woman's direction, but when he said, "Thank you," he looked at Carrie.

"So . . ." Rocky stuck his hands in his pockets. His fingers found the little tissue-wrapped package he'd tucked away that morning. A tremble filled his middle, and he had to force a smile. "Do you have anything special to do right now?"

Carrie lifted her wrist and checked her watch. "Hmm . . . no pressing engagements I can think of." She lifted her head and peeked up at him. "Why? Did you have something in mind?"

Oh yes, he had something in mind all right. He licked his lips. "Thought maybe we'd swing by Elmwood Towers." His pounding heart made him seek a temporary diversion. "Maybe see how Eileen is doing."

She offered a quick nod. "That sounds fine. I haven't talked to her in several weeks."

They headed out of the building together, and Rocky kept his hands in his pockets. He wanted to hold her hand again, but his palms felt all sweaty, and he was afraid they'd give him away. But he did allow his elbow to brush her arm occasionally, and each time he did it she glanced up at him. The smiles that flew between them increased the tempo of his heartbeats with each connection.

Carrie leaned back on the headrest and closed her eyes as he drove to Elmwood Towers. He knew she wasn't asleep — her eyelids twitched — but he decided not to disturb her. She looked so peaceful, so content. Gratitude hit like an ocean wave. How readily she trusted him — her relaxed pose told him that more clearly than words could have. *Thank You, God, for the changes You've created in me. Thank You for helping me feel worthy of this woman. . . .*

The moment he shut off the ignition, Carrie opened her eyes and smiled in his direction. "Ready?"

"Yep. Let's go." This time he took her hand. He couldn't help it — she rounded the car and held her hand toward him, an expression of expectation on her face. Before he took it, however, he swiped his own palm down his pantleg to remove any moisture.

Swinging their hands between them, he guided her to Tower Three, and they rode the elevator to the fifth floor. Their knock on Eileen's door went unanswered. Rocky consulted his wristwatch. "Hmm . . . I wonder if she met some friends for lunch and is chatting."

Carrie released a light laugh. "If so, it may be a while before she returns. Eileen does enjoy visiting."

Rocky's heart pounded. Carrie was right — it could be an hour or more before Eileen returned. Well, no time with Eileen meant no more delays. He might as well get to it. He raised his shoulders in a shrug. "Well, we're here. Want to . . . go sit on our bench?"

"Sure." Carrie slipped her hand into the bend of his elbow. On the elevator she leaned her forehead against his shoulder for a moment, her eyes closed in contentment. Again Rocky was struck with the trust she placed in him. He vowed from that moment forward never to do anything that would make her regret giving him her trust.

Carrie seated herself on the bench and lifted her face to him. The sun above the flowering pear tree crept between leaves and created dappled shadows across her cheeks. Rocky longed to kiss each splash of shade. He swallowed hard.

"Are you going to sit down?"

He gave a start, realizing he still stood beside the bench. "Oh! Yeah, sure, I'll sit." Stiffly he bent his knees and perched beside her. He wished his heart would settle down. Any minute it might boom right out of his chest. Maybe he should get this over with; yet he wanted to do things right. Carrie deserved things done right.

"Rocky, are you okay?"

The concern in her tone made him reach for her hand. "I'm fine. I'm just . . ." He chuckled, rubbing his finger beneath his nose in an attempt to stop the quiver in his upper lip. "I just want to tell you something, and I'm looking for the right words."

"Do you need me to sit quietly and not bother you?"

He looked into her sweet face, saw the love and acceptance shining in her eyes, and suddenly he knew exactly what to do. Cupping her cheeks with both hands, he leaned forward and placed a tender kiss on her soft lips.

She released a little gasp, but then her hands came up to clasp his wrists. Tears appeared, trembling on her thick lower lashes, reminding Rocky of dewdrops on rose petals. He brushed the droplets away with his thumbs.

"Carrie, I love you. You already knew that, didn't you?" He heard his husky tone, felt the emotion rumble beneath the words.

She drew in her breath, her face still held within his palms. Although she didn't speak, he saw the answer in her eyes. She knew.

Slowly he released her face. Slipping from the bench, he knelt in front of her and reached into his pocket. His gaze never wavered from her eyes as he removed the little package and began peeling back the paper.

The slight crackle of tissue paper underscored his words. "Carrie Mays, I believe God has grown a love in my heart for you that will endure throughout eternity. You would make me the happiest man on the planet if you would do me the honor of becoming my wife."

From the wad of paper he lifted the slim gold band he'd chosen. Sun filtered through the tree branches overhead, lighting the diamond set within a circle of prongs. Carrie gasped as he took her left hand and slid the ring onto her finger. She stared at the ring, and tears splashed down her cheeks past the curve of her smile.

Finally she met his gaze, her blue eyes bright with more unshed tears. "I love you, too, Rocky. I would be honored to become your wife." She slipped from the bench to melt into his arms. They clung, hearts pounding in unison, for long seconds, each absorbing the moment, memorizing it, celebrating it.

Finally Rocky pulled back to lift her onto the bench once more. He settled himself beside her then lifted her hand to kiss the knuckle of the finger that wore the ring. He held her hand out in front of them and drew in a deep breath. "It looks perfect there."

"It is perfect there," she agreed on a breathy sigh.

A hint of regret wiggled down his spine as he looked at the simple ring. "Stone's not as big as I wanted, but —"

"Don't ever apologize, Rocky." She tugged at his hand until he met her gaze. "You chose this for me, and it's perfect for me. Just as you are perfect for me."

He shook his head, the wonder striking again. Carrie . . . Carrie loved him. It was as hard to fathom as God loving him. Yet he accepted it. He drew her into his arms once more. "I love you, Carrie."

"I know."

She rested her chin on his shoulder, and although she embraced him he knew only one arm was wrapped around his back. He chuckled. "Are you peeking at that ring?"

Pulling free, she laughed. "How did you know?"

He imitated her position, hugging her

while extending one arm straight out from her back, which showed her how he'd known. She laughed again, the joy in the laughter making Rocky's heart skip a beat. He planted another quick kiss on her laughing lips. Taking her hands, he captured her attention.

"Carrie, I can't guarantee we'll live like kings, but I do promise you your needs will always be met."

"Oh, I know." She sighed, her soft smile lighting her eyes. "Rocky, I've told you again and again that I have no desire to live like kings. Having my needs met is all I could ask for." Her smile turned coquettish. "And right now all I need is another kiss."

He obliged her willingly, and suddenly the sound of applause intruded. They pulled apart and looked over their shoulders then burst into laughter.

Lined up on the sidewalk stood Eileen and her boys — John, Martin, and Tim — each smacking their palms together with enthusiasm and smiling brightly enough to rival the sun.

"Rocky, we saw you kissing!" John covered his mouth with his hands, his shoulders shaking with laughter.

Rocky gave Carrie a sheepish look, but she merely shrugged and grinned.

"Do I hear wedding bells?" Eileen called.

John looked at her in surprise. "There are no bells, Eileen. That is clapping you hear. Right, Martin and Tim?"

The other two men nodded solemnly, and Eileen's laughter joined that of Rocky and Carrie. Taking Carrie by the hand, Rocky jogged across the grass. He wrapped Eileen in a bear hug while Carrie looked on and Eileen's boys snickered.

Rocky whispered in Eileen's ear, "She said yes."

And Eileen whispered back, "I'm not surprised. She's a smart girl — knows a good catch when she sees one."

Rocky gave Eileen's wrinkled cheek a kiss then pulled away to wrap an arm around Carrie's waist. "Yes, you definitely heard wedding bells," he announced, "and all of you will be invited to the wedding. Which will be . . . ?" He looked at Carrie.

She smiled up at him. "In the early spring, when the tulips you are going to plant in our backyard are in full bloom. I want tulips in every color of the rainbow. And we'll recite our vows in the yard, with our friends" — her gaze swept over Eileen and the boys — "and family close by." Leaning her head against his shoulder, she sighed. "And then we'll show everyone the meaning of living happily ever after."

Epilogue

Carrie peeked out the kitchen to the backyard, where guests mingled on the grassy carpet. Some stood in small groups along the walking path that gently curved through the garden area, which showcased hundreds of plump tulips at full bloom. Her eyes feasted on the splashes of bright color — every color of the rainbow, just as she'd asked.

The yard would be Rocky's best advertisement for his landscaping business. The arrangement of tulips was perfectly balanced, undeniably eye-catching. He'd created a walking path of concrete stepping stones, each of which bore a different insect — from butterflies to bumblebees — formed with broken pottery, glass chips, and marbles. She could see guests pointing, nodding, admiring.

She winged a quick prayer of thankfulness heavenward for this perfect spring day.

Kansas could be unpredictable in the spring so, just in case, they had decorated the living room in preparation for an indoor wedding. But the weather was ideal — warm but not hot, breezy but not windy. A beautiful, sunshiny, Kansas day. Being outside on the manicured lawn with its profusion of color was exactly what Carrie had envisioned, and she rejoiced at the culmination of her dream-come-true wedding.

Her eyes sought and found Rocky, and she stifled a giggle. There he was, on his wedding day, plucking something that didn't belong from between the leafy tulips. She shook her head — gardening was most certainly in his blood. He would be successful in his business venture. She had no doubt.

Pride welled in her chest as she thought about everything he had accomplished in the past several months. In addition to completing his first semester of college and making the dean's honor roll, he had tilled the ground around his trailer and planted seedlings of various flowering trees. Although nothing else was growing out there, he had a blueprint of plans for the remainder of the ground.

After today he would no longer live in his trailer house — her heart caromed at that thought — and he had plans to turn the trailer into his office. She smiled as she remembered him saying, "A man needs a place to call his own. I won't clutter up our yard and house here with all my stuff — it can stay out there, and that will be my playground." She knew he would keep his playground neat and orderly. He took such pride in everything he did.

With a sigh Carrie turned from the window to find Eileen in the kitchen doorway, watching her with a smile on her wrinkled face. Carrie laughed self-consciously.

"You caught me peeking."

Eileen crossed the floor to join Carrie. "Yes, I did, but I don't believe in that bad-luck-to-see-the-groom-before-the-wedding nonsense." She rose up on tiptoe to peek outside. "He looks awfully handsome, doesn't he?"

Carrie looked again, her heart rising into her throat at the sight of Rocky with his brother, Philip, talking with the minister. "Oh yes," she released on a breathy sigh. "He's very handsome."

Rocky had said, somewhat apologetically, that a formal wedding wasn't his comfort zone. Could they do something simple? And Carrie had cheerfully agreed. Instead of a tuxedo, Rocky wore a neatly pressed pair of pleated navy trousers with a crisp white button-down shirt — she chuckled to herself — with sleeves intact. His tie lifted in the breeze, and he caught it, smoothing it down across his taut stomach. The muted colors of the tie included all the colors of the tulips, and he blended in perfectly with his surroundings.

Her eyes drifted to his hair, which he had insisted on having trimmed for this day, but to her relief he hadn't cropped the waves that touched the top edge of his collar. She loved those sun-kissed curls.

"It's nearly time," Eileen said softly. "Are you ready?"

For a moment Carrie's chest pinched. Among the guests were her mother and Myrna, but Mac hadn't come. He remained adamantly opposed to Carrie taking up with "that Wilder boy" and refused to witness the union. His stubbornness put a tinge of sadness on an otherwise perfect day, but she wouldn't allow Mac to be a rain cloud on her wedding.

She pressed her hands to her tummy for a moment as nervous excitement roused a flurry of butterflies. "Yes, I'm ready. At least I think I am. Do I look okay?"

Eileen's gaze traveled from Carrie's tumbling blond curls down the length of her pink lace dress, ending with her white high-heeled sandals. The woman's smile grew as her gaze returned to Carrie's eyes. "Honey, you're perfect. You'll take Rocky's breath away."

"That's good," Carrie quipped, "because I seem to have none of my own!" Her heart beat at twice its normal rhythm, and her words came out in breathless gasps.

Eileen's forehead creased. "Scared?"

Carrie processed what she was feeling. She shook her head. "No, I'm not afraid. I'm eager."

Eileen nodded in approval. "That's just what you're supposed to feel. C'mon, Carrie — let's go."

Through the open sliding door piano music gently wafted from the CD player. Eileen handed Carrie her bouquet of tulips, their stems bound with an abundance of curling pink ribbon, then slipped out the garage door to join the others in the yard.

Carrie stepped through the sliding door. Guests, standing on the grass, turned to watch her progress. But Carrie was barely aware of their presence — her focus was on Rocky who waited beside the minister at the edge of the tulip garden. His brown-eyed gaze pinned to hers, a smile grew on his face. The joy in his expression brought a great rush of eagerness to Carrie's heart, and it was all she could do to keep from running across the yard and catapulting into his arms.

But Carrie forced her feet to move evenly, steadily, toward her groom, matching the relaxed beat of the music. Her heart celebrated. *Lord, thank You for answering my prayer for a man who would love me for myself. Your gifts are perfect.*

When she was within two yards of Rocky she could no longer maintain the slow progress, and she skipped the final few feet, her face upturned, her smile so wide she could feel the rounding of her cheeks.

They had written their own vows — simple, straightforward promises from the heart. The minister read a brief passage of scripture — First Corinthians 13 — and advised the couple to make the words a part of their lives. Less than fifteen minutes from the time Carrie stepped through the sliding door, the minister presented them to their waiting guests as man and wife.

Rocky's arms wrapped around Carrie's waist, lifting her off the ground, and his lips found hers. Her own arms looped around his neck, holding him tight. When the kiss ended, they laughed into one another's faces while applause broke around them.

Rocky let her feet slip to the ground, but he still held her close as he whispered, "Today is the bud, Carrie. We have the rest of our lives to make the bloom. We are going to create the most beautiful blossom the world has ever seen."

She shook her head, laughing softly. "You just can't leave gardening for one moment, can you?"

"I can't leave God's plan for me," he corrected her, tapping the end of her nose with his finger. "And I'm so happy you're a part of it."

She nestled into his arms. "Oh, me, too, Rocky. Me, too."

They released one another to receive the congratulations and hugs of their guests. When everyone had partaken of the cake and punch and left for home, Rocky and Carrie walked arm-in-arm along the path. Dusk was falling, throwing rosy shadows across the lawn and deepening the colors of the tulips. Rocky sat on the bench in the back corner of the yard, Carrie curled beside him, her head cradled against his shoulder.

"So, Mrs. Wilder. . . ." Rocky's arm was tucked snug around her waist, his thumb tracing a lazy circle on her hip. "How does it feel to be Mrs. Wilder instead of Miss Mays?"

"Wonderful." Carrie twisted her head to deliver a kiss on the underside of his jaw. His hand tightened on her waist.

"I'm still in awe." His low-voiced comment captured Carrie's attention. "It all seems kind of like someone else's life, you know?"

Carrie understood what he meant. "I know. Who would have thought someone would love Carrie enough to look past the money to the person?"

"Who would have thought someone would love Rocky enough to look past 'that Wilder boy' to the man he's become?"

Relishing the feel of her husband's arms wrapped securely around her, Carrie released a contented sigh. "That's the wonder of God, isn't it? He makes all things new."

Rocky didn't reply, but she felt his kiss on the top of her head. Then he rose, tugging her to her feet. His brown eyes crinkled into a warm smile as he took her hand. "C'mon, Mrs. Wilder. Let's go get started on that happily ever after."

ABOUT THE AUTHOR

Kim Vogel Sawyer, a Kansas resident, is a wife, mother, grandmother, teacher, writer, speaker, and lover of cats and chocolate. From the time she was a very little girl, she knew she wanted to be a writer, and seeing her words in print is the culmination of a lifelong dream. Kim relishes her time with family and friends and stays active in her church by teaching adult Sunday School, singing in the choir, and being a "ding-a-ling" (playing in the bell choir). In her spare time, she enjoys drama, quilting, and calligraphy. She welcomes visitors to her Web site at www.KimVogelSawyer.com

The employees of Thorndike Press hope you have enjoyed this Large Print book. All our Thorndike and Wheeler Large Print titles are designed for easy reading, and all our books are made to last. Other Thorndike Press Large Print books are available at your library, through selected bookstores, or directly from us.

For information about titles, please call:
(800) 223-1244

or visit our Web site at:
http://gale.cengage.com/thorndike

To share your comments, please write:
Publisher
Thorndike Press
295 Kennedy Memorial Drive
Waterville, ME 04901